THE GRAPHIC NOVEL
Charlotte Brontë

ORIGINAL TEXT VERSION

Script Adaptation: Amy Corzine
Artwork: John M. Burns
Lettering: Terry Wiley
Associate Editor: Joe Sutliff Sanders
Design & Layout: Jo Wheeler & Carl Andrews
Publishing Assistant: Joanna Watts
Additional Information: Karen Wenborn

Editor in Chief: Clive Bryant

Jane Eyre: The Graphic Novel
Original Text Version

Charlotte Brontë

First US edition published: December 2008
Reprinted: April 2011, October 2016

Library bound edition published: October 2016

Published by: Classical Comics Ltd
Copyright ©2008 Classical Comics Ltd.

All enquiries should be addressed to:
Classical Comics Ltd.
PO Box 177
LUDLOW
SY8 9DL
United Kingdom

info@classicalcomics.com
www.classicalcomics.com

Paperback ISBN: 978-1-906332-47-1
Library bound ISBN: 978-1-907127-41-0

Printed in the USA.

This book is printed by CG Book Printers using environmentally safe inks, on paper from responsible sources. This material can be disposed of by recycling, incineration for energy recovery, composting and biodegradation.

The publishers would like to acknowledge the design assistance of Greg Powell in the completion of this book.

The rights of Amy Corzine, John M. Burns, Terry Wiley and Joe Sutliff Sanders to be identified as the artists of this work have been asserted in accordance with the Copyright, Designs and Patents Act 1988 sections 77 and 78.

Contents

❧ ❧

❧ ❧

Dramatis Personae

Jane Eyre

Mr. Edward Fairfax Rochester
Owner of Thornfield Hall

Young Jane Eyre

Mr. Reed
Jane's uncle

Mrs. Sarah Reed
Jane's aunt

John Reed
Jane's cousin

Eliza Reed
Jane's cousin

Georgiana Reed
Jane's cousin

Miss Bessie Lee
Maid at Gateshead Hall

Miss Abbott
Maid at Gateshead Hall

Mr. Lloyd
Apothecary

Mr. Brocklehurst
Manager of Lowood School

Miss Maria Temple
*Superintendent at
Lowood School*

Helen Burns
*Jane's friend at
Lowood School*

Miss Alice Fairfax
Housekeeper at
Thornfield Hall

Adèle Varens
Jane's pupil

Céline Varens
Adèle's mother

Grace Poole
Servant at Thornfield Hall

Lord Ingram

Lady Ingram

Miss Blanche Ingram
Daughter of Lord and
Lady Ingram

Miss Mary Ingram
Daughter of Lord and
Lady Ingram

Bertha Mason
Rochester

Richard Mason
Bertha's brother

Mr. Briggs
A solicitor from London

Pilot
Mr. Rochester's dog

St. John Rivers

Mary Rivers
Sister to St. John

Diana Rivers
Sister to St. John

Rosamond Oliver
Friend of St. John Rivers

The Birth of Jane Eyre

Charlotte Brontë's *Jane Eyre* was a huge success when it first appeared in 1847. It was a year of great achievement for the Brontë sisters of Haworth: the publication of Anne Brontë's *Agnes Grey*, and Emily Brontë's *Wuthering Heights* also taking place that same year.

That success, however, was set against a family history full of loss and sadness.

Despite the many advances made in medical science during the nineteenth century, potentially fatal diseases were still extremely common. Charlotte had to cope with her mother's death when she was only five years old; and then, four years later, two of her sisters were lost to tuberculosis.

Young Charlotte was fortunate enough to have a caring father and aunt to look after her — but what about an infant who had lost both parents?

It was usual for orphaned children to be looked after by relatives; and while the kindness of that act cannot be denied, the emotional impact of the loss of parents on the child, coupled with the stresses felt by the family looking after an extra person in the household, could provide the background to an unhappy childhood — especially for a poor, plain little girl, thrust into the home of her spiteful cousins and an uncaring aunt.

Jane Eyre

~ PROLOGUE ~

NORTHERN ENGLAND IN THE EARLY NINETEENTH CENTURY

NOW THAT *TYPHUS* HAS FELLED BOTH MY *SISTER* AND HER *HUSBAND*, WE MUST LOOK AFTER THEIR *CHILD*.

REVEREND EYRE

WIFE TO REVEREND EYRE

GATESHEAD HALL

ONE YEAR LATER...

PROMISE ME, MRS. REED, TO REAR AND MAINTAIN LITTLE *JANE EYRE* AS ONE OF OUR *OWN* CHILDREN.

I *WILL*, HUSBAND.

~ CHAPTER I ~

NINE YEARS LATER...

NO LONG **WALK** TODAY, SO NO **NIPPED FINGERS** AND **TOES.**

I REGRET TO KEEP YOU AT A **DISTANCE,** JANE,

BUT UNTIL I HAVE HEARD FROM THE **NURSEMAID, BESSIE** --

I **LIKE** IT WHEN **BESSIE** TELLS ME **STORIES**

-- THAT YOU ARE **ENDEAVOURING** IN **GOOD EARNEST** TO ACQUIRE A MORE **SOCIABLE** AND **CHILDLIKE DISPOSITION** --

-- A MORE **ATTRACTIVE** AND **SPRIGHTLY MANNER**

- SOMETHING **LIGHTER, FRANKER,** MORE **NATURAL** -

I REALLY **MUST** EXCLUDE YOU FROM **PRIVILEGES** INTENDED ONLY FOR **CONTENTED, HAPPY** LITTLE CHILDREN.

WHAT DOES BESSIE SAY I HAVE **DONE?**

JANE, I DON'T LIKE **CAVILLERS** OR **QUESTIONERS;** BESIDES, THERE IS SOMETHING TRULY **FORBIDDING** IN A **CHILD** TAKING UP HER **ELDERS** IN THAT MANNER.

BE SEATED SOMEWHERE; AND UNTIL YOU CAN SPEAK **PLEASANTLY,** REMAIN **SILENT.**

BOH! MADAM MOPE!...

WHERE THE DICKENS IS SHE?

IT IS WELL I DREW THE CURTAIN

LIZZY! GEORGY!

JOAN* IS NOT HERE:

TELL MAMA SHE IS RUN OUT INTO THE RAIN --

-- BAD ANIMAL!

SHE IS IN THE WINDOW-SEAT, TO BE SURE, JACK.

WHAT DO YOU WANT?

SAY: "WHAT DO YOU WANT, MASTER REED?"

THAT WAS THE ANSWER!

I WANT YOU TO COME HERE --

-- THAT IS FOR YOUR IMPUDENCE IN ANSWERING MAMA A WHILE BACK --

SMACK

-- AND FOR YOUR SNEAKING WAY OF GETTING BEHIND CURTAINS, AND FOR THE LOOK YOU HAD IN YOUR EYES TWO MINUTES SINCE, YOU RAT!

WHAT WERE YOU DOING BEHIND THE CURTAIN?

I WAS READING.

10

*Master Reed would often call her Jo

SHOW THE **BOOK.** --

-- YOU HAVE NO **BUSINESS** TO TAKE OUR **BOOKS;**

YOU ARE A **DEPENDENT,** MAMA SAYS; YOU HAVE NO **MONEY.** YOU OUGHT TO **BEG,** NOT LIVE WITH **GENTLEMAN'S CHILDREN** LIKE **US,** AND EAT THE SAME **MEALS** WE DO, AND WEAR **CLOTHES** AT OUR **MAMMA'S EXPENSE** --

-- **NOW** I'LL TEACH YOU TO RUMMAGE MY **BOOKSHELVES,** FOR THEY ARE **MINE. ALL** THE HOUSE BELONGS TO ME, OR **WILL DO.**

GO AND STAND BY THE **DOOR,** OUT OF THE WAY OF THE **MIRROR** AND THE **WINDOWS.**

AAH!

THUMP!

WICKED AND **CRUEL BOY!**

YOU ARE LIKE A **MURDERER,** A **SLAVE-DRIVER** --

-- YOU ARE LIKE THE **ROMAN EMPERORS!**

WHAT! WHAT! DID YOU **HEAR** HER, **ELIZA** AND **GEORGIANA?**

WON'T I TELL **MAMA!** BUT **FIRST** --

RAT! RAT!

MAMA! MAMA!

DEAR, DEAR! WHAT A **FURY** TO FLY AT **MASTER JOHN!**

DID **ANYBODY** SEE SUCH A **PICTURE** OF **PASSION?**

TAKE HER AWAY TO THE **RED-ROOM** AND **LOCK HER** IN THERE.

~ CHAPTER II ~

FOR **SHAME,** FOR **SHAME!**

WHAT **SHOCKING CONDUCT,** MISS EYRE, TO **STRIKE** YOUR YOUNG **MASTER!**

MASTER! HOW IS HE MY **MASTER?** AM I A **SERVANT?**

NO, YOU ARE **LESS** THAN A SERVANT, FOR YOU DO **NOTHING** FOR YOUR **KEEP.**

YOU OUGHT **NOT** TO THINK YOURSELF ON **EQUALITY** WITH THE **MISSES REED** AND **MASTER** REED, BECAUSE **MISSIS** KINDLY ALLOWS YOU TO BE **BROUGHT UP** WITH THEM.

THEY WILL HAVE A **GREAT DEAL** OF **MONEY** AND YOU WILL HAVE **NONE**. IT IS YOUR **PLACE** TO MAKE YOURSELF **AGREEABLE** TO THEM.

WHAT WE TELL YOU IS FOR YOUR **OWN GOOD**.

IF **MRS. REED** WERE TO **TURN YOU OUT**, YOU WOULD HAVE TO GO TO THE **POORHOUSE**.

COME BESSIE, WE WILL **LEAVE** HER --

-- I WOULDN'T HAVE HER **HEART** FOR **ANYTHING**.

SAY YOUR **PRAYERS, MISS EYRE,** WHEN YOU ARE BY **YOURSELF**; FOR IF YOU DON'T **REPENT**, SOMETHING **BAD** MIGHT BE PERMITTED TO COME DOWN THE **CHIMNEY** AND **FETCH YOU AWAY**.

UNJUST! - UNJUST!

HUH?!?

SHREEIK!!

TAKE ME **OUT**!

LET ME GO INTO THE **NURSERY**!

BANG! BANG! BANG!

WELL, WHO AM I?

MR. LLOYD...

~ CHAPTER III ~

...THE APOTHECARY THAT MRS. REED USES FOR HER SERVANTS. HER FAMILY GET A PHYSICIAN.

WE SHALL DO VERY WELL, BY AND BY.

WOULD YOU LIKE TO DRINK, OR COULD YOU EAT ANYTHING?

NO, THANK YOU, BESSIE. WHAT IS THE MATTER WITH ME? AM I ILL?

YOU FELL SICK, I SUPPOSE, IN THE RED-ROOM WITH CRYING; YOU'LL BE BETTER SOON; NO DOUBT. YOU MAY CALL ME IF YOU WANT ANYTHING IN THE NIGHT. I WILL BE SLEEPING NEXT DOOR.

NEXT MORNING...

WELL, YOU HAVE BEEN CRYING, MISS JANE EYRE: CAN YOU TELL ME WHAT ABOUT? HAVE YOU ANY PAIN?

NO, SIR.

I DARESAY SHE IS CRYING BECAUSE SHE COULD NOT GO OUT WITH MISSIS IN THE CARRIAGE.

SURELY NOT! WHY, SHE IS TOO OLD FOR SUCH PETTISHNESS.

I NEVER **CRIED** FOR SUCH A THING IN MY **LIFE**. I **HATE** GOING OUT IN THE **CARRIAGE**. I **CRY** BECAUSE I AM **MISERABLE**.

OH **FIE**, MISS!

WHAT MADE YOU **ILL** YESTERDAY?

SHE HAD A **FALL**.

A **FALL**! THAT IS LIKE A **BABY** AGAIN!

CAN'T SHE MANAGE TO **WALK** AT **HER** AGE? SHE MUST BE **EIGHT** OR **NINE** YEARS **OLD**.

I WAS KNOCKED **DOWN**... BUT **THAT** DID NOT MAKE ME **ILL**.

THAT BELL IS FOR **YOU**, NURSE.

RING!!!

YOU CAN GO DOWN FOR YOUR **DINNER** NOW. I WILL GIVE **MISS JANE** A **LECTURE** UNTIL YOU COME **BACK**.

THE **FALL** DID NOT MAKE YOU ILL. WHAT **DID**, THEN?

I WAS **SHUT UP** IN A **ROOM** WHERE THERE IS A **GHOST**, TILL AFTER **DARK**.

GHOST! WHAT? YOU **ARE** A **BABY** AFTER **ALL**! YOU ARE **AFRAID** OF **GHOSTS**?

OF **MR. REED'S** GHOST I **AM**.

HE **DIED** IN THAT ROOM AND WAS **LAID OUT** THERE.

NO-ONE GOES INTO IT AT **NIGHT** IF THEY CAN **HELP** IT; AND IT WAS **CRUEL** TO SHUT ME UP **ALONE** WITHOUT A **CANDLE** --

-- SO **CRUEL** I THINK I SHALL **NEVER FORGET** IT.

15

NONSENSE! AND IS IT *THAT* MAKES YOU SO MISERABLE *NOW*? ARE YOU *AFRAID* NOW IN DAYLIGHT?

NO, BUT *NIGHT* WILL COME *AGAIN* BEFORE LONG -

AND BESIDES -

I AM *UNHAPPY*, *VERY* UNHAPPY, FOR *OTHER* THINGS.

WHAT OTHER THINGS?

I HAVE NO *MOTHER*, *BROTHERS* OR *SISTERS*.

YOU HAVE A KIND *AUNT* AND *COUSINS*...

BUT *JOHN REED* KNOCKED ME *DOWN* AND MY *AUNT* SHUT ME UP IN THE *RED-ROOM*.

HAVE YOU ANY RELATIONS *BESIDES* MRS. REED?

I DON'T *KNOW*. I ASKED AUNT REED ONCE, AND SHE SAID POSSIBLY I MIGHT HAVE SOME *POOR*, *LOW* RELATIONS CALLED *EYRE*, BUT SHE KNEW *NOTHING* ABOUT THEM.

IF YOU *HAD* SUCH, WOULD YOU LIKE TO GO TO *THEM*?

NO, I SHOULD *NOT* LIKE TO BELONG TO *POOR* PEOPLE.

POVERTY TO ME WAS *SYNONYMOUS* WITH *DEGRADATION*.

WOULD YOU LIKE TO GO TO *SCHOOL*?

I SHOULD *INDEED* LIKE TO GO TO SCHOOL.

WELL, WELL; WHO KNOWS *WHAT* MAY HAPPEN?

THE *CHILD* OUGHT TO HAVE A *CHANGE OF AIR* AND *SCENE* - NERVES NOT IN A GOOD *STATE*.

THEY THINK I AM *ASLEEP*.

MISSIS WAS, SHE *DARED* SAY, *GLAD ENOUGH* TO GET *RID* OF SUCH A *TIRESOME, ILL-CONDITIONED* CHILD, WHO ALWAYS LOOKED AS IF SHE WERE *WATCHING* EVERYBODY AND *SCHEMING* PLOTS UNDERHAND.

HER *MOTHER* MARRIED THAT *POOR CLERGYMAN* AGAINST THE WISHES OF HER *FRIENDS*, WHO THOUGHT HIM *BENEATH* HER, AND OF HER *FATHER* MR. *REED* --

-- WHO *CUT HER OFF* WITHOUT A *SHILLING*.

THEN, BUT MARRIED A *YEAR*, THE *CLERGYMAN* CAUGHT THE *TYPHUS FEVER* WHILE VISITING AMONG THE *POOR* --

-- HER *MOTHER* THEN CAUGHT IT FROM *HIM* AND *BOTH* DIED WITHIN A *MONTH* OF EACH *OTHER*.

POOR MISS *JANE* IS TO BE PITIED *TOO*, ABBOTT.

YES, IF SHE WERE A *NICE, PRETTY* CHILD; BUT ONE REALLY *CANNOT* CARE FOR SUCH A LITTLE *TOAD* AS THAT.

~ CHAPTER IV ~

SOME WEEKS LATER...

Ma-mah says not to speak to the creature.

WHACK

WAHHH!

MA-MAH, THAT NASTY *JANE EYRE* HAS **FLOWN** AT ME LIKE A **MAD CAT!**

DON'T TALK TO *ME* ABOUT HER, *JOHN.*

I **TOLD** YOU NOT TO GO **NEAR** HER.

SHE IS **NOT WORTHY** OF **NOTICE.**

I **DO NOT** CHOOSE THAT EITHER *YOU* OR YOUR **SISTERS** SHOULD **ASSOCIATE** WITH HER.

THEY ARE NOT **FIT** TO ASSOCIATE WITH **ME!**

DO NOT **RISE** FROM THAT **SPOT** OR UTTER **ONE** SYLLABLE FOR THE **REST** OF THE **DAY.**

WHAT WOULD **UNCLE REED** SAY TO YOU, IF HE WERE **ALIVE?**

MY **UNCLE REED** IS IN **HEAVEN**, AND CAN **SEE** ALL YOU **DO** AND **THINK**; AND SO CAN **PAPA** AND **MAMMA**:

THEY **KNOW** HOW YOU **SHUT ME UP** ALL DAY LONG AND WISH ME **DEAD**.

WHAT?

SLAP!

NOVEMBER, DECEMBER AND HALF OF **JANUARY** PASSED AWAY. **CHRISTMAS** AND THE **NEW YEAR** WERE CELEBRATED AT GATESHEAD WITH THE USUAL **FESTIVE CHEER**; **PRESENTS** HAD BEEN INTERCHANGED; **DINNERS** AND **EVENING PARTIES** GIVEN.

FROM **EVERY ENJOYMENT**, I WAS **EXCLUDED**.

ON THE **FIFTEENTH** OF **JANUARY**, I WAS CALLED TO **MRS. REED**...

THIS IS THE **LITTLE GIRL** RESPECTING WHOM I **APPLIED** TO YOU.

HER **SIZE** IS **SMALL**. WHAT IS HER **AGE?**

TEN YEARS.

YOUR **NAME**, LITTLE GIRL?

JANE EYRE, SIR.

ARE YOU A **GOOD** CHILD?

PERHAPS THE **LESS** SAID ON **THAT** SUBJECT THE **BETTER**, MR. BROCKLEHURST.

19

DO YOU **KNOW** WHERE THE **WICKED** GO AFTER **DEATH**?

AND WHAT **IS** HELL?

THEY GO TO **HELL**.

A **PIT** FULL OF **FIRE**.

WHAT MUST YOU **DO** TO **AVOID** IT?

I MUST KEEP IN **GOOD** HEALTH, AND **NOT** DIE.

CHILDREN **YOUNGER** THAN **YOU** DIE **DAILY**.

MR. **BROCKLEHURST**, THIS LITTLE GIRL IS NOT **QUITE** THE **CHARACTER** AND **DISPOSITION** I COULD **WISH**; SHE MUST BE **WATCHED CLOSELY** TO GUARD AGAINST HER **WORST FAULT** – A **TENDENCY** TO **DECEIT**.
I WISH HER TO BE MADE **USEFUL**, KEPT **HUMBLE**, BROUGHT UP IN A **MANNER** SUITING HER **PROSPECTS**, AND TO SPEND **ALL VACATIONS** AT **LOWOOD SCHOOL**.

HUMILITY IS A **CHRISTIAN GRACE**.

I **MORTIFY** PUPILS AT LOWOOD AGAINST THE **WORLDLY SENTIMENT** OF **PRIDE**.

AFTER **VISITING** MY **SCHOOL**, MY **SECOND** DAUGHTER, **AUGUSTA**, EXCLAIMED:

HOW **QUIET** AND **PLAIN** THE GIRLS LOOK – LIKE **POOR PEOPLE'S CHILDREN**.

THEY LOOKED AT MY **DRESS** AND **MAMMA'S** AS IF THEY HAD **NEVER** SEEN A **SILK GOWN** BEFORE.

HAD I SOUGHT **ALL ENGLAND** OVER, I COULD **SCARCELY** HAVE FOUND A SYSTEM MORE **EXACTLY** FITTING A **CHILD** LIKE **JANE EYRE**.

NO **DOUBT**, NO **DOUBT**, MADAM.

GO OUT OF THE **ROOM**. RETURN TO THE **NURSERY**.

IF I WERE **DECEITFUL**, I WOULD SAY I **LOVED** YOU.

BUT I DECLARE I *DO NOT* LOVE YOU.

HOW *DARE* YOU, *JANE* EYRE!

HOW *DARE I?* BECAUSE IT IS THE *TRUTH.* YOU HAVE NO PITY.

I AM *GLAD* YOU ARE *NO RELATION* OF MINE.

I'LL *NEVER* CALL YOU *AUNT* AGAIN AS *LONG* AS I LIVE.

THE VERY *THOUGHT* OF YOU MAKES ME *SICK.*

I SHALL *REMEMBER* YOUR *PUNISHMENT* OF ME WHEN YOUR *WICKED BOY* KNOCKED ME *DOWN* FOR *NOTHING.*

PEOPLE THINK YOU *GOOD,* BUT YOU ARE *BAD.*

YOU ARE DECEITFUL.

JANE, WHAT IS THE *MATTER* WITH YOU? WOULD YOU LIKE SOME *WATER?*

NO, MRS. REED.

I *ASSURE* YOU, I DESIRE TO BE YOUR *FRIEND.*

NOT *YOU.* YOU TOLD MR. BROCKLEHURST I HAD A *BAD CHARACTER,* A *DECEITFUL DISPOSITION.* I'LL LET *EVERYBODY* AT LOWOOD KNOW WHAT YOU *ARE* AND WHAT YOU HAVE *DONE.*

JANE, YOU DON'T *UNDERSTAND* THESE THINGS.

CHILDREN MUST BE *CORRECTED* FOR THEIR *FAULTS.*

DECEIT IS NOT MY *FAULT.*

BUT YOU ARE *PASSIONATE.* THAT YOU MUST *ALLOW.*

NOW *RETURN* TO THE *NURSERY* - THERE'S A DEAR. *LIE DOWN* A LITTLE.

I AM *NOT* YOUR *DEAR.* I *CANNOT* LIE DOWN.

SEND ME TO *SCHOOL* SOON, MRS. REED, FOR I *HATE* TO *LIVE* HERE.

I WILL **INDEED** SEND HER TO **SCHOOL** SOON.

I STOOD THERE **ALONE**, **WINNER** OF THE **FIELD**, AND ENJOYED MY **CONQUEROR'S SOLITUDE**.

A CHILD CANNOT **QUARREL** WITH ITS **ELDERS** WITHOUT EXPERIENCING THE **PANG** OF **REMORSE**.

BUT THIS FIERCE PLEASURE **SUBSIDED** IN ME AS FAST AS DID MY **PULSES**.

HALF AN HOUR'S **REFLECTION** SHOWED ME THE **MADNESS** OF MY **CONDUCT**.

BESSIE **COMFORTED ME** THAT AFTERNOON, TELLING ME HER MOST ENCHANTING **STORIES** AND **SINGING** HER **SWEETEST SONGS**.

YOU ARE A **STRANGE** CHILD, **JANE**... A LITTLE **ROVING, SOLITARY** THING.

WON'T YOU BE **SORRY** TO LEAVE POOR **BESSIE?**

WHAT DOES **BESSIE** CARE? SHE IS ALWAYS **SCOLDING** ME.

BECAUSE YOU'RE SUCH A **QUEER, FRIGHTENED, SHY** LITTLE THING YOU SHOULD BE **BOLDER.**

WHAT? TO GET MORE **KNOCKS?**

NONSENSE!

EVEN FOR **ME**, LIFE HAD ITS **GLEAMS OF SUNSHINE.**

FIVE O'CLOCK HAD BARELY *STRUCK* ON THE NINETEENTH OF JANUARY WHEN *BESSIE* BROUGHT A CANDLE INTO MY CLOSET, AND FOUND ME *ALREADY DRESSING* BY THE LIGHT OF A JUST-SETTING *HALF-MOON.*

~ CHAPTER V ~

WILL YOU GO IN AND BID MISSIS GOODBYE?

NO, BESSIE: SHE CAME TO MY *CRIB* LAST NIGHT AND SAID I NEED NOT *DISTURB* HER IN THE MORNING, NOR MY *COUSINS* EITHER;

AND SHE TOLD ME TO SAY SHE HAD BEEN MY *BEST FRIEND.*

WHAT DID *YOU* SAY, MISS?

NOTHING. I COVERED MY *FACE* WITH THE *BEDCLOTHES* AND TURNED FROM *HER* TO THE *WALL.*

THAT WAS *WRONG,* MISS *JANE.*

IT WAS QUITE *RIGHT,* BESSIE. YOUR *MISSIS* HAS NOT BEEN MY *FRIEND.* SHE HAS BEEN MY *FOE.*

GOODBYE TO GATESHEAD!

THE DAY SEEMED TO ME OF *PRETERNATURAL LENGTH,* AND WE *APPEARED* TO TRAVEL OVER *HUNDREDS OF MILES OF ROAD.*

I HAD *AT LAST* DROPPED *ASLEEP* WHEN THE SUDDEN *CESSATION* OF MOTION AWOKE ME.

IS THERE A *LITTLE GIRL* HERE CALLED JANE EYRE?

YES

THE **CHILD** IS VERY **YOUNG** TO BE SENT **ALONE**. SHE HAD BETTER BE **PUT TO BED** SOON; SHE LOOKS **TIRED**.

ARE YOU **TIRED?**

A **LITTLE,** MA'AM

AND **HUNGRY TOO,** NO DOUBT.

LET HER HAVE SOME **SUPPER** BEFORE SHE GOES TO **BED,** MISS **MILLER.**

I WAS CHANGED INTO MY **UNIFORM** AND TAKEN INTO A **WIDE, LONG ROOM.**

MONITORS, COLLECT THE **LESSON-BOOKS** AND PUT THEM AWAY!

MONITORS, FETCH THE **SUPPER-TRAYS!**

24

THE **MEAL** OVER, **PRAYERS** WERE READ BY **MISS MILLER**, AND THE CLASS **FILED OFF**, TWO AND TWO, UPSTAIRS. EACH **BED** WAS FILLED WITH **TWO OCCUPANTS**, AND **TO-NIGHT** I WAS TO BE **MISS MILLER'S** BED-FELLOW.

THE **NIGHT** PASSED **RAPIDLY** AND WE WERE **AWOKEN** BY A **LOUD BELL**.

Disgusting! The **porridge** is **burnt** again!

SILENCE!

WHY IS EVERYONE STANDING? I HAD HEARD NO **ORDER** GIVEN.

IT WAS THE **SUPERINTENDENT** OF **LOWOOD**, MISS **TEMPLE**.

YOU HAD THIS **MORNING** A **BREAKFAST** YOU COULD NOT **EAT**. YOU MUST BE **HUNGRY**.

I HAVE **ORDERED** THAT A **LUNCH** OF **BREAD AND CHEESE** BE SERVED TO **ALL**.

BREAD AND **CHEESE!** WE ARE HAVING **LUNCH!**

25

"LOWOOD INSTITUTION ... REBUILT BY NAOMI BROCKLEHURST OF BROCKLEHURST HALL ...'LET YOUR LIGHT SO SHINE BEFORE MEN THAT THEY MAY SEE YOUR GOOD WORKS AND GLORIFY YOUR FATHER WHICH IS IN HEAVEN.' - ST. MATTHEW, VERSE 16."

COUGH!

IS YOUR BOOK **INTERESTING**?

I **LIKE** IT.

WHAT IS IT **ABOUT**?

YOU MAY **LOOK** AT IT.

THIS LOOKS **DULL**. NOTHING ABOUT **FAIRIES** OR **GENII**.

CAN YOU **TELL** ME, WHAT **IS** LOWOOD INSTITUTION?

THIS **HOUSE** WHERE YOU ARE COME TO **LIVE**. IT IS PARTLY A **CHARITY SCHOOL** FOR EDUCATING **ORPHANS**.

CHARITY? DO WE PAY NO **MONEY**?

WE **PAY**, OR OUR **FRIENDS** PAY, FIFTEEN POUNDS A YEAR.

THEN **WHY** DO THEY CALL US **CHARITY CHILDREN**?

BECAUSE **FIFTEEN POUNDS** IS **NOT ENOUGH** FOR **BOARD** AND **TEACHING**.

THE **DEFICIENCY** IS SUPPLIED BY BENEVOLENT-MINDED **LADIES** AND **GENTLEMEN**.

IS HE A **GOOD** MAN, MR. **BROCKLEHURST?**

HE IS A **CLERGYMAN,** AND IS SAID TO DO A **GREAT DEAL** OF **GOOD.**

BUT **MISS TEMPLE** IS THE **BEST** - ISN'T SHE?

SHE IS **ABOVE** THE **REST.**

HAVE YOU BEEN **LONG** HERE?

TWO YEARS.

ARE YOU **HAPPY** HERE?

YOU ASK **RATHER TOO MANY QUESTIONS.** I HAVE GIVEN YOU **ANSWERS ENOUGH** FOR THE PRESENT. **NOW** I WANT TO **READ.**

~ CHAPTER VI ~

THE NEXT **MORNING** WE COULD NOT **WASH** AS THE **WATER** IN THE PITCHERS WAS **FROZEN.** LATER THAT **AFTERNOON,** MY **NEW FRIEND** BECAME THE **SUBJECT OF ATTENTION...**

YOU **DIRTY, DISAGREEABLE GIRL!** YOU HAVE **NEVER CLEANED** YOUR **NAILS** THIS MORNING!

WHY DOES SHE NOT **EXPLAIN** THAT SHE COULD NEITHER **CLEAN** HER **NAILS** NOR **WASH** HER FACE, AS THE **WATER** WAS **FROZEN?**

HARDENED GIRL! NOTHING CAN CORRECT YOU OF YOUR **SLATTERNLY HABITS:**

CARRY THE **ROD AWAY.**

THAT EVENING...

YOU MUST WISH TO **LEAVE** LOWOOD.

NO, WHY **SHOULD** I? I WAS **SENT HERE** TO GET AN **EDUCATION.**

BUT THAT **TEACHER,** MISS SCATCHERD, IS SO **CRUEL** TO YOU!

CRUEL? NOT AT **ALL.** SHE IS **SEVERE.** SHE **DISLIKES** MY **FAULTS.**

IF **I** WERE IN **YOUR** PLACE I SHOULD **DISLIKE** HER. IF SHE **STRUCK** ME WITH THAT **ROD,** I SHOULD **BREAK IT** UNDER HER **NOSE.**

IF YOU **DID,** MR. **BROCKLEHURST** WOULD **EXPEL YOU.**

IT IS FAR **BETTER** TO ENDURE **PATIENTLY** A **SMART** WHICH **NOBODY** FEELS BUT **YOURSELF.**

IF PEOPLE WERE ALWAYS **KIND** AND **OBEDIENT** TO THOSE WHO ARE **CRUEL** AND **UNJUST**, THE **WICKED** PEOPLE WOULD HAVE IT **ALL THEIR OWN WAY;**

THEY WOULD NEVER FEEL **AFRAID**, AND THEY WOULD NEVER **ALTER**.

WHEN WE ARE **STRUCK AT** WITHOUT A **REASON**, WE SHOULD **STRIKE BACK** AGAIN VERY **HARD** - SO HARD AS TO **TEACH** THE PERSON WHO **STRUCK** US NEVER TO DO IT **AGAIN**.

IT IS AS **NATURAL** AS **LOVING** THOSE WHO SHOW US **AFFECTION**.

HEATHENS AND **SAVAGE TRIBES** HOLD THAT DOCTRINE. BUT **CIVILISED** NATIONS **DISOWN** IT.

IT IS NOT **VIOLENCE** THAT BEST OVERCOMES **HATE**, NOR **VENGEANCE** THAT MOST CERTAINLY HEALS **INJURY** --

-- **READ** THE **NEW TESTAMENT** AND OBSERVE HOW **CHRIST** ACTS. MAKE HIS **WORD** YOUR **RULE** AND HIS **CONDUCT** YOUR **EXAMPLE**.

WHAT DOES HE **SAY?**

LOVE YOUR **ENEMIES. BLESS** THEM THAT **CURSE** YOU. DO **GOOD** TO THEM THAT **HATE** AND **USE YOU**.

THEN I SHOULD **LOVE** MRS. **REED**, WHICH I **CANNOT** DO. I SHOULD **BLESS** HER SON **JOHN**, WHICH IS **IMPOSSIBLE**.

I PROCEEDED TO **POUR OUT** THE TALE OF MY **SUFFERINGS**, SPEAKING AS I **FELT**, WITHOUT **RESERVE** OR **SOFTENING**. **HELEN** HEARD ME **PATIENTLY** TO THE **END**.

MRS. **REED** WAS **UNKIND** TO YOU BECAUSE SHE **DISLIKES** YOUR **CAST OF CHARACTER**, AS MISS **SCATCHERD** DOES MINE.

BUT HOW **MINUTELY** YOU REMEMBER EVERYTHING!

WOULD YOU NOT BE **HAPPIER** IF YOU TRIED TO **FORGET** HER SEVERITY AND YOUR **PASSIONATE EMOTIONS**?

LIFE APPEARS TO **ME** TOO **SHORT** TO BE SPENT IN NURSING **ANIMOSITY**. WE ARE ALL **BURDENED** WITH **FAULTS**.

SOON WE SHALL **PUT OFF** OUR **CORRUPTIBLE** BODIES AND ONLY THE **SPARK** OF OUR **SPIRIT** WILL **REMAIN**.

I CAN SINCERELY **FORGIVE** THE **CRIMINAL** WHILE I **ABHOR** THE **CRIME**.

REVENGE NEVER **WORRIES** MY **HEART** AND **DEGRADATION** NEVER TOO DEEPLY **DISGUSTS** ME. I LIVE IN **CALM**, LOOKING TO THE **END**.

~ CHAPTER VII ~

MY **FIRST QUARTER** AT **LOWOOD** SEEMED AN **AGE**, AND NOT THE **GOLDEN AGE** EITHER ...

29

JANUARY...

...WITH THE **KEEN APPETITES** OF **GROWING CHILDREN**, WE WERE FED SCARCELY **SUFFICIENT** TO KEEP **ALIVE** A **DELICATE INVALID**...

...WHENEVER THE **FAMISHED GREAT GIRLS** HAD AN **OPPORTUNITY**, THEY WOULD **COAX** OR **MENACE** THE **LITTLE ONES** OUT OF **THEIR** PORTION...

...ONE **AFTERNOON** (I HAD BEEN **THREE WEEKS** AT **LOWOOD**), THE **MOMENT** I HAD **DREADED** ARRIVED...

...I WAS **SURE** MR. **BROCKLEHURST** WAS ABOUT TO **FULFILL** HIS **PROMIS** TO MRS. **REED** TO DISCLOSE MY **VICIOUS NATURE** TO MISS **TEMPLE** AND THE **TEACHERS**.

...AND SHE IS **NOT**, ON **ANY ACCOUNT**, TC GIVE OUT **MORE** THAN **ONE DARNING NEEDL** AT A **TIME** TO EACH PUPIL.

A **LUNCH** OF **BREAD** AND **CHEESE** HAS **TWICE** BEEN SERVED DURING THE PAST **FORTNIGHT**.

NO SUCH MEAL AS LUNCH IS **ALLOWED**. WHO **INTRODUCED** THIS INNOVATION? AND BY WHAT **AUTHORITY**?

I MUST BE **RESPONSIBLE**, SIR. THE **BREAKFAST** WAS SO **ILL-PREPARED** THAT THEY COULD NOT **POSSIBLY** EAT IT; AND I **DARED** NOT ALLOW THEM TO REMAIN **FASTING** TILL DINNER-TIME.

MADAM, MY **PLAN** IS NOT TO **ACCUSTOM** THEM TO HABITS OF **LUXURY** AND **INDULGENCE**, BUT TO **RENDER** THEM **HARDY, PATIENT, SELF-DENYING.**

A **JUDICIOUS INSTRUCTOR** WOULD TAKE THE **OPPORTUNITY** OF REFERRING TO THE **SUFFERINGS** OF THE **PRIMITIVE CHRISTIANS;** THAT **MAN** SHALL NOT **LIVE** BY **BREAD** ALONE.

WHEN YOU PUT **BREAD** AND **CHEESE** INSTEAD OF **BURNT PORRIDGE** INTO CHILDREN'S MOUTHS, YOU MAY FEED THEIR **VILE BODIES,** BUT **HOW** YOU STARVE THEIR **IMMORTAL SOULS!**

...MISS **TEMPLE**, WHAT IS THAT **GIRL** WITH **CURLED HAIR?** RED HAIR, MA'AM, **CURLED** ALL **OVER?**

IT IS **JULIA SEVERN.** HER HAIR CURLS **NATURALLY.**

I **DESIRE** THE **HAIR** TO BE **ARRANGED CLOSELY, MODESTLY, PLAINLY.**

TELL ALL THE **FIRST FORM** TO DIRECT THEIR **FACES** TO THE **WALL.**

ALL THOSE **TOP-KNOTS** MUST BE **CUT OFF.**

BUT **SIR** -

MADAM, MY **MISSION** IS TO **MORTIFY** THE **LUSTS OF THE FLESH,** TO **TEACH** THESE GIRLS TO **CLOTHE** THEMSELVES WITH **SHAME-FACEDNESS,** AND **SOBRIETY,**

NOT WITH **BRAIDED HAIR** AND **COSTLY APPAREL.**

MRS. **BROCKLEHURST,** WELCOME. PLEASE, DO SIT **DOWN,** YOU AND YOUR **DAUGHTERS.**

CRASH!

A CARELESS GIRL!

IT IS THE **NEW PUPIL**, I PERCEIVE. I HAVE A **WORD** TO SAY RESPECTING **HER**.

LET THE CHILD WHO BROKE HER **SLATE** COME **FORWARD**.

Don't be *afraid*, Jane, I saw it was an *accident*; you shall *not* be punished.

ANOTHER **MINUTE**, AND SHE WILL **DESPISE** ME FOR A HYPOCRITE.

LADIES, MISS TEMPLE, TEACHERS AND CHILDREN, YOU ALL SEE THIS **GIRL**?

OBSERVE SHE POSSESSES THE **ORDINARY** FORM OF **CHILDHOOD** GRACIOUSLY GIVEN TO HER BY **GOD**.

WHO WOULD **THINK** THAT THE **EVIL ONE** HAD **ALREADY** FOUND A **SERVANT** AND **AGENT** IN HER?

How shocking!

BE ON **GUARD** AGAINST HER. **AVOID** HER COMPANY. **TEACHERS**, SCRUTINISE HER ACTIONS, PUNISH HER **BODY** TO **SAVE** HER SOUL. THIS GIRL IS —

A LIAR!

HER **PIOUS, CHARITABLE BENEFACTRESS** TOLD ME THIS **UNHAPPY ORPHAN** REPAID HER WITH **INGRATITUDE**. LET HER STAND HALF AN HOUR **LONGER** ON THAT **STOOL**, AND LET **NO ONE** SPEAK TO HER DURING THE **REMAINDER** OF THE DAY.

THERE WAS I, THEN, **EXPOSED** TO GENERAL VIEW ON A PEDESTAL OF **INFAMY**. WHAT MY **SENSATIONS** WERE, **NO LANGUAGE** CAN DESCRIBE. A GIRL PASSED ME AND LIFTED HER **EYES**.

WHAT AN **EXTRAORDINARY SENSATION** THAT RAY SENT THROUGH ME.

MISS **SCATCHERD** CONDEMNED **HELEN BURNS** TO A DINNER OF **BREAD** AND **WATER** BECAUSE SHE **BLOTTED** A PAGE WITH **INK**.

UNTIDY

SUCH **SPOTS** ARE ON THE **DISC** OF THE **CLEAREST PLANET**, AND EYES LIKE MISS **SCATCHERD'S** CAN ONLY SEE THOSE **MINUTE DEFECTS**, AND ARE **BLIND** TO THE **FULL BRIGHTNESS** OF THE **ORB**.

~ CHAPTER VIII ~

ERE THE HALF HOUR ENDED, *FIVE O'CLOCK* STRUCK; SCHOOL WAS *DISMISSED*, AND ALL WERE *GONE* INTO THE *REFECTORY* FOR TEA.

LEFT TO *MYSELF,* I *WEPT;* AND MY *TEARS* WATERED THE *BOARDS.*

COME, EAT SOMETHING.

HELEN, WHY DO YOU *STAY* WITH A GIRL WHOM *EVERYONE* BELIEVES TO BE A *LIAR?*

EVERYBODY, JANE? ONLY *EIGHTY PEOPLE* HAVE HEARD YOU CALLED SO. THE WORLD CONTAINS *HUNDREDS* OF *MILLIONS.*

THE *EIGHTY* I KNOW *DESPISE* ME.

JANE, PROBABLY NOT *ONE* IN THE SCHOOL *DESPISES* OR *DISLIKES* YOU. MR. *BROCKLEHURST* IS NOT A *GOD.* NOR IS HE EVEN *LIKED* HERE.

IF OTHERS DON'T *LOVE ME,* I WOULD RATHER *DIE* THAN *LIVE.* I CANNOT *BEAR* TO BE SOLITARY AND *HATED,* HELEN.

HUSH, JANE! YOU THINK *TOO MUCH* OF THE *LOVE* OF HUMAN *BEINGS.* BESIDES THIS *EARTH* AND THE RACE OF *MEN,* THERE IS AN *INVISIBLE WORLD* AND A *KINGDOM OF SPIRITS.*

ANGELS SEE OUR *TORTURES* AND *RECOGNISE* OUR *INNOCENCE* --

≶ COUGH ≶

I *CAME* ON PURPOSE TO *INVITE YOU* TO MY *ROOM,* JANE EYRE. AS *HELEN BURNS* IS WITH YOU, SHE MAY COME *TOO.*

WE SHALL *THINK* YOU WHAT YOU *PROVE YOURSELF* TO BE, MY *CHILD.* CONTINUE TO ACT AS A *GOOD GIRL,* AND YOU WILL *SATISFY US.*

NOW *TELL ME,* WHO IS THE *LADY* WHOM MR. *BROCKLEHURST* CALLED YOUR *BENEFACTRESS?*

MRS. *REED,* MY *UNCLE'S* WIFE.

MY *UNCLE* IS *DEAD,* AND HE LEFT ME TO HER *CARE.*

DID MRS. REED NOT **ADOPT** YOU OF HER **OWN** ACCORD?

NO, MA'AM. THE **SERVANTS** SAID THAT MY **UNCLE** GOT HER TO **PROMISE** BEFORE HE **DIED** THAT SHE WOULD ALWAYS **KEEP** ME.

THEN I TOLD HER THE STORY OF MY **SAD CHILDHOOD,** OF THE **RED-ROOM** AND MY **FIT** - IN THE COURSE OF WHICH I MENTIONED **MR. LLOYD.**

I HAVE **HEARD** SOMETHING OF MR. LLOYD AND SHALL **WRITE** TO HIM. IF HIS **REPLY** AGREES WITH YOUR STATEMENT, YOU SHALL BE **PUBLICLY CLEARED** FROM EVERY **IMPUTATION.**

TO **ME, JANE,** YOU ARE **CLEAR** NOW.

HOW **ARE** YOU TO-NIGHT, **HELEN?** HAVE YOU **COUGHED** MUCH TODAY?

NOT **QUITE** SO MUCH, I THINK, MA'AM.

MISS TEMPLE SHOWED **GENUINE** CONCERN FOR US. AFTER SHE GAVE US A **SUPPER TREAT** OF TEA, TOAST AND CAKE, THE BELL ANNOUNCED OUR **BEDTIME** AND WE LEFT HER WITH A **TEAR** ON HER **CHEEK.**

ABOUT A **WEEK LATER** AT A **SCHOOL ASSEMBLY...**

AN **ENQUIRY** WAS MADE INTO THE **CHARGES** AGAINST **JANE EYRE,** AND I AM **MOST HAPPY** TO **PRONOUNCE** THAT SHE HAS BEEN **CLEARED** OF **EVERY ACCUSATION** MADE **AGAINST** HER.

~ CHAPTER IX ~

THE **HARDSHIPS** OF LOWOOD **LESSENED** AS **SPRING** DREW ON. MY WRETCHED **FEET, FLAYED** AND **SWOLLEN** TO **LAMENESS** BY THE **SHARP AIR** OF JANUARY, BEGAN TO **HEAL.**

LOWOOD SHOOK **LOOSE** ITS **TRESSES.** IT BECAME ALL **FLOWERY** WITH **SNOW-DROPS, CROCUSES, PURPLE AURICULAS, LILIES, ROSES, WILD PRIMROSES** AND **GOLDEN-EYED PANSIES.**

ITS GREAT **ELM, ASH,** AND **OAK SKELETONS** WERE **RESTORED** TO **MAJESTIC LIFE.**

BUT THAT **FOREST-DELL**, WHERE **LOWOOD** LAY, WAS THE **CRADLE** OF **FOG** AND **FOG-BRED PESTILENCE**;

WHICH, **QUICKENING** WITH THE QUICKENING **SPRING**, BREATHED **TYPHUS** INTO THE **ORPHAN ASYLUM**.

FORTY-FIVE OUT OF THE **EIGHTY** GIRLS LAY **ILL**.

CLASSES WERE **BROKEN UP** AND **RULES** WERE **RELAXED**. MISS **TEMPLE'S** WHOLE **ATTENTION** WAS ABSORBED BY THE **PATIENTS** AND SHE **LIVED** IN THE **SICK ROOM**.

MANY GIRLS, ALREADY SMITTEN, **WENT HOME** ONLY TO **DIE**. **SOME DIED** AT THE **SCHOOL**, **AND** WERE BURIED **QUIETLY** AND **QUICKLY**; THE NATURE OF THE **MALADY** FORBIDDING **DELAY**.

ENQUIRIES WERE MADE INTO THE **SCANDAL**...

SEMI-STARVATION AND NEGLECTED **COLDS** HAVE **PREDISPOSED** MOST OF THE **PUPILS** TO **INFECTION**.

NOT TO **MENTION** THEIR **THIN CLOTHING**, AND **WRETCHED ACCOMMO-DATION**.

AND THE **FETID WATER** IN THE **COOKING POTS**.

WERE THEY FED AT **ALL**, MR. **BROCKLEHURST?** I UNDERSTAND THAT YOU **BANNED LUNCH**.

HELEN WAS **ILL** AT PRESENT; FOR SOME WEEKS SHE HAD BEEN REMOVED FROM SIGHT. FINALLY HER **NURSE** TOLD ME **HELEN'S** BED WAS IN MISS **TEMPLE'S** ROOM, AS SHE HAD **CONSUMPTION**, NOT **TYPHUS**. SHE TOLD ME THAT I COULD **NOT SEE HER**, BUT I **CREPT** INTO HER ROOM AFTER ELEVEN.

Helen, are you **awake?**

WHY ARE YOU **COME** HERE, **JANE?** IT IS PAST **ELEVEN O'CLOCK.**

I CAME TO SEE **YOU**, HELEN. I HEARD YOU WERE VERY **ILL** AND I **COULD NOT SLEEP** TILL I HAD **SPOKEN** TO YOU.

YOU CAME TO BID ME **GOODBYE**, THEN. YOU ARE **JUST IN TIME**, PROBABLY.

ARE YOU **GOING HOME**, HELEN?

YES, TO MY **LAST** HOME.

NO, NO, HELEN!

≷COUGH≷

≷COUGH!!≷

≷COUGH!!!≷

JANE, YOUR LITTLE **FEET** ARE **BARE**. LIE DOWN AND **COVER** YOURSELF WITH MY **QUILT.**

I AM VERY **HAPPY**, JANE, AND WHEN YOU HEAR THAT I AM **DEAD**, YOU MUST BE SURE AND **NOT GRIEVE**. THERE IS **NOTHING** TO GRIEVE **ABOUT.**

BY DYING **YOUNG**, I SHALL ESCAPE GREAT **SUFFERINGS**. I HAD NOT **QUALITIES** OR **TALENTS** TO MAKE MY WAY VERY **WELL** IN THE **WORLD.**

BUT WHERE ARE YOU **GOING TO**, HELEN?

I AM **GOING** TO GOD.

LATER I LEARNED THAT **MISS TEMPLE** HAD **FOUND ME** THE NEXT MORNING, MY **ARMS** ROUND HELEN'S **NECK**. I WAS **ASLEEP**, AND HELEN WAS - **DEAD.**

~ CHAPTER X ~

AFTER *TYPHUS* DIED AWAY, WEALTHY BENEVOLENT INDIVIDUALS INTRODUCED *IMPROVEMENTS* IN *DIET, CLOTHING* AND *BUILDINGS* AT LOWOOD SCHOOL, AND MANAGEMENT BY *COMMITTEE.* MR. BROCKLEHURST BECAME *TREASURER,* SUPERVISED BY GENTLEMEN OF RATHER MORE *ENLARGED* AND *SYMPATHETIC* MINDS.

I REMAINED AN *INMATE* OF ITS WALLS FOR *EIGHT YEARS. SIX* AS A PUPIL, AND *TWO* AS A TEACHER.

I WAS *HAPPY* AS A *TEACHER* AT LOWOOD, BUT MY *TRANQUILLITY* DEPARTED WITH *MISS TEMPLE.*

YOU ARE NO LONGER *MOTHER, GOVERNESS* AND *COMPANION* TO ME - BUT *MRS. NASMYTH,* WIFE OF A *CLERGYMAN.*

FARE YOU *WELL!*

FARE *YOU* WELL, DEAREST *JANE.*

I *TIRED* OF THE ROUTINE OF *EIGHT YEARS* IN ONE AFTERNOON. I DESIRED *LIBERTY;* FOR *LIBERTY* I UTTERED A *PRAYER;* IT SEEMED *SCATTERED* ON THE *WIND* THEN FAINTLY BLOWING, SO I ASKED FOR *CHANGE, STIMULUS.* EVEN *THAT* SEEMED SWEPT OFF INTO A *VAGUE SPACE...*

...THEN, *GRANT ME* AT *LEAST A NEW SERVITUDE!*

I PLACED AN *ADVERTISEMENT* FOR MY *SERVICES* IN THE *HERALD NEWSPAPER.*

I RECEIVED ONLY *ONE* RESPONSE TO MY ADVERTISEMENT, FROM A MRS. *FAIRFAX* IN *THORNFIELD.* I ACCEPTED THE POST OF *GOVERNESS* IN HER HOUSE...

... AND ON THE *MORNING* OF MY *DEPARTURE,* I RECEIVED A *VISITOR.*

WELL, WHO *IS IT?*

YOU'VE NOT *QUITE* FORGOTTEN *ME,* I THINK, MISS JANE?

BESSIE!

BESSIE!

BESSIE!

MY LITTLE **BOY** HERE IS CALLED **BOBBY,** AND I'VE A LITTLE **GIRL** THAT I'VE CHRISTENED **JANE.**

I'VE BEEN **MARRIED** NEARLY **FIVE YEARS** TO THE **COACHMAN.**

AND YOU DON'T LIVE IN **GATESHEAD?**

I LIVE AT THE **LODGE:** THE **OLD PORTER** HAS **LEFT.**

TELL ME **EVERYTHING,** BESSIE.

LAST **WINTER,** A YOUNG **LORD** FELL IN LOVE WITH **MISS GEORGIANA,** BUT HIS **RELATIONS** WERE **AGAINST** THE MATCH; **AND** - WHAT DO YOU **THINK?** - HE AND MISS GEORGIANA MADE IT UP TO **RUN AWAY.**

MISS **ELIZA** FOUND THEM **OUT** AND **STOPPED** IT. I BELIEVE SHE WAS **ENVIOUS.**

NOW **SHE** AND HER **SISTER** LEAD A **CAT** AND **DOG** LIFE TOGETHER; THEY ARE ALWAYS **QUARRELLING.**

JOHN REED IS **NOT** DOING SO **WELL** AS HIS **MAMA** COULD **WISH.** HE WENT TO **COLLEGE** TO STUDY THE **LAW:**

BUT HE IS **SUCH A DISSIPATED YOUNG MAN,** THEY WILL **NEVER** MAKE **MUCH** OF HIM, I THINK.

AND **MRS. REED?**

MISSIS **LOOKS** STOUT AND WELL ENOUGH, BUT SHE'S **NOT QUITE** EASY IN HER **MIND.**

MR. **JOHN'S** CONDUCT DOES **NOT** PLEASE HER - HE **SPENDS** A DEAL OF **MONEY.**

DID **SHE** SEND YOU HERE, **BESSIE?**

NO INDEED; BUT I HAVE **LONG WANTED** TO **SEE** YOU, AND WHEN I **HEARD** THAT YOU WERE GOING TO **ANOTHER PART** OF THE **COUNTRY,**

I THOUGHT I'D GET A **LOOK** AT YOU BEFORE YOU WERE **QUITE** OUT OF MY **REACH.**

I **ALSO** LEARNED THAT AN **UNCLE** HAD CALLED TO GATESHEAD SEVEN YEARS AGO ASKING ABOUT ME. HE WAS DISAPPOINTED NOT TO SEE ME, AND HE HAD TO **LEAVE** FOR MADEIRA.

I WAS COLLECTED FROM THE *GEORGE INN* AT *MILLCOTE* BY A *PLAIN SERVANT* IN A *PLAIN CARRIAGE. THORNFIELD* WAS A SHORT *SIX MILES* AWAY.

WILL YOU **WALK** THIS **WAY,** MA'AM?

~ CHAPTER XI ~

MRS. **FAIRFAX,** I SUPPOSE?

YES, YOU ARE **RIGHT:** DO SIT **DOWN.**

I **DARESAY** YOUR **HANDS** ARE ALMOST **NUMBED** WITH **COLD.**

-- **LEAH,** MAKE A LITTLE **HOT HEGUS** AND CUT A **SANDWICH** OR TWO.

DRAW **NEARER** TO THE **FIRE.**

SHE TREATS ME LIKE A **VISITOR.** THIS IS **NOT** LIKE WHAT I HAVE HEARD OF THE TREATMENT OF **GOVERNESSES.**

SHALL I HAVE THE PLEASURE OF SEEING MISS FAIRFAX **TO-NIGHT?**

WHAT DID YOU SAY MY **DEAR?** OH, YOU MEAN MISS **VARENS!**

THEN SHE IS NOT YOUR **DAUGHTER?**

NO - I HAVE **NO** FAMILY.

I AM **SO** GLAD YOU ARE **COME;** IT WILL BE QUITE **PLEASANT** LIVING HERE NOW WITH A **COMPANION.**

BUT I'LL NOT KEEP YOU SITTING UP **LATE** TO-NIGHT, IT IS ON THE **STROKE** OF TWELVE NOW.

39

I'VE HAD THE **ROOM** NEXT TO **MINE** PREPARED FOR YOU.

I THOUGHT YOU WOULD LIKE IT **BETTER** THAN ONE OF THE **LARGER** CHAMBERS: THEY ARE SO **DREARY** AND **SOLITARY**.

NEXT **MORNING**...

THORNFIELD IS A VERY **PRETTY** PLACE.

YES IT **IS;**

BUT I FEAR IT WILL BE GETTING **OUT OF ORDER,** UNLESS **MR. ROCHESTER** SHOULD RESIDE HERE **PERMANENTLY.**

MR. **ROCHESTER!** WHO IS **HE?**

THE **OWNER** OF **THORNFIELD.** DID YOU NOT **KNOW** HE WAS CALLED **ROCHESTER?**

I THOUGHT **THORNFIELD** BELONGED TO **YOU.**

TO **ME?** BLESS **YOU,** CHILD, WHAT AN **IDEA!** I AM ONLY THE **HOUSEKEEPER** - THE **MANAGER.**

AND THE LITTLE **GIRL** - MY **PUPIL?**

SHE IS MR. ROCHESTER'S **WARD.**

SO MUCH THE **BETTER** - MY **POSITION** HERE IS ALL THE **FREER.**

HERE SHE **COMES,** WITH HER **"BONNE"** AS SHE CALLS HER **NURSE.**

GOOD **MORNING,** MISS **ADÈLE.** COME AND SPEAK TO THE **LADY** WHO IS TO **TEACH YOU.**

C'EST LA MA GOUVERANTE!

MAIS OUI, CERTAINEMENT.

40

ARE THEY **FOREIGNERS?**

THE **NURSE** IS A FOREIGNER AND **ADÈLE** WAS BORN ON THE **CONTINENT;** AND, I BELIEVE, NEVER **LEFT IT** TILL WITHIN **SIX MONTHS AGO.**

I DON'T **UNDERSTAND** HER, SHE MIXES **ENGLISH** SO WITH **FRENCH.**

I LIVED **LONG AGO** WITH **MAMA,** BUT SHE IS GONE TO THE **HOLY VIRGIN.**

MAMA USED TO TEACH ME TO **DANCE** AND SING, AND TO SAY VERSES. A GREAT MANY GENTLEMEN AND LADIES CAME TO SEE **MAMA.**

I USED TO **DANCE** BEFORE THEM, OR SIT ON THEIR **KNEES** AND SING TO THEM.

AFTER **BREAKFAST, ADÈLE** AND I WITHDREW TO THE **LIBRARY.**

I FOUND MY PUPIL SUFFICIENTLY **DOCILE,** THOUGH **DISINCLINED** TO **APPLY:** SHE HAD NOT BEEN USED TO **REGULAR OCCUPATION** OF **ANY KIND.**

WHEN THE MORNING HAD ADVANCED TO **NOON,** I ALLOWED HER TO RETURN TO HER **NURSE.**

LATER, MRS. **FAIRFAX** SHOWED ME AROUND THE **HOUSE.**

IN WHAT **ORDER** YOU KEEP THESE **ROOMS,** MRS. **FAIRFAX!**

WHY, THOUGH **MR. ROCHESTER'S** VISITS ARE **RARE,** THEY ARE ALWAYS **SUDDEN** AND **UNEXPECTED.**

DO YOU **LIKE** HIM?

OH **YES;** THE **FAMILY** HAVE ALWAYS BEEN **RESPECTED** HERE.

SOME OF THE **THIRD-STOREY ROOMS** WERE **INTERESTING** FROM THEIR AIR OF **ANTIQUITY,** GIVING THE ASPECT OF A **HOME** OF THE **PAST** - A **SHRINE** OF **MEMORY.**

IF THERE WERE A **GHOST** AT **THORNFIELD HALL,** THIS WOULD BE ITS **HAUNT.**

SO I **THINK.**

YOU **HAVE** NO **GHOST,** THEN?

NONE THAT **I** EVER HEARD OF.

I FOLLOWED STILL, UP A VERY NARROW STAIRCASE TO THE ATTICS, AND THENCE BY A LADDER AND THROUGH A TRAP-DOOR TO THE ROOF OF THE HALL.

I WAS NOW ON A LEVEL WITH THE CROW COLONY AND COULD SEE INTO THEIR NESTS.

I PROCEEDED TO DESCEND WHEN...

AH-HA-HA...

MRS. FAIRFAX! DID YOU HEAR THAT LOUD LAUGH? WHO IS IT?

SOME OF THE SERVANTS, VERY LIKELY.

PERHAPS GRACE POOLE.

TOO MUCH NOISE, GRACE. REMEMBER DIRECTIONS!

WHO IS GRACE POOLE?

SHE IS A PERSON WE HAVE TO SEW AND ASSIST LEAH IN HER HOUSEMAID'S WORK; NOT ALTOGETHER UNOBJECTIONABLE IN SOME POINTS, BUT SHE DOES WELL ENOUGH.

THREE MONTHS *LATER*, IN *JANUARY*, MRS. *FAIRFAX* HAD JUST WRITTEN A *LETTER* WHICH WAS WAITING TO BE *POSTED*, SO I VOLUNTEERED TO *CARRY IT* TO *HAY*: THE *DISTANCE*, TWO MILES, WOULD BE A PLEASANT WINTER AFTERNOON *WALK*.

~ CHAPTER XII ~

A *RUDE NOISE* BROKE: A *HORSE* WAS COMING...

WHOO-OOSH!!

ROWF! ROWF!

WHAT THE *DEUCE* IS *TO DO* NOW?

ROWF! ROWF!

DOWN, PILOT!

IF YOU ARE *HURT*, AND WANT *HELP*, SIR, I CAN *FETCH* SOMEONE EITHER FROM *THORNFIELD HALL* OR FROM *HAY*.

I HAVE NO **BROKEN BONES** - ONLY A **SPRAIN**.

WHERE DO YOU **COME** FROM?

FROM JUST **BELOW**; I WILL RUN OVER TO **HAY** FOR YOU WITH **PLEASURE** IF YOU **WISH** IT; INDEED I AM **GOING THERE** TO POST A **LETTER**.

I SHOULD THINK **YOU** OUGHT TO BE AT HOME **YOURSELF**.

DO YOU COME FROM THAT **HOUSE** WITH THE **BATTLEMENTS**?

YES, SIR. I AM THE **GOVERNESS**.

AH, THE **GOVERNESS** -

DEUCE TAKE ME IF I HAD NOT **FORGOTTEN**! THE **GOVERNESS**!

EXCUSE ME - **NECESSITY** COMPELS ME TO MAKE YOU **USEFUL**.

HE LAID A **HEAVY HAND** ON MY **SHOULDER** AND **LIMPED** TO HIS **HORSE**.

THANK YOU. NOW **MAKE HASTE** WITH THE LETTER TO **HAY**, AND **RETURN** AS FAST AS YOU **CAN**.

A **TOUCH** OF A **SPURRED HEEL** MADE HIS HORSE FIRST **START** AND **REAR**, AND THEN **BOUND AWAY**.

LIKE **HEATH** THAT, IN THE **WILDERNESS**, THE **WILD WIND** WHIRLS **AWAY**.

IT WAS AN INCIDENT OF **NO MOMENT**, YET IT MARKED WITH CHANGE ONE **SINGLE HOUR** OF **MONOTONOUS LIFE**. MY HELP HAD BEEN **NEEDED** AND **CLAIMED**.

TRANSITORY THOUGH THE DEED WAS, IT WAS YET AN **ACTIVE** THING, AND I WAS **WEARY** OF AN EXISTENCE ALL **PASSIVE**.

I DID NOT LIKE **RE-ENTERING** THORNFIELD. TO PASS ITS **THRESHOLD** WAS TO RETURN TO **STAGNATION**.

LEAH, WHAT **DOG** IS THIS?

HE CAME WITH **MASTER** -

MR. ROCHESTER

- HE IS JUST **ARRIVED**.

JOHN IS GONE FOR A **SURGEON**, FOR **MASTER** HAS HAD AN **ACCIDENT**. HIS **HORSE** SLIPPED ON SOME **ICE** IN **HAY LANE**.

44

ADÈLE WAS NOT EASY TO **TEACH** THE NEXT DAY; SHE COULD NOT **APPLY.** SHE KEPT **RUNNING** TO THE **DOOR** AND LOOKING TO SEE IF SHE COULD GET A **GLIMPSE** OF **MR. ROCHESTER.**

~ CHAPTER XIII ~

LATER IN THE **AFTERNOON,** MRS. **FAIRFAX** CAME IN.

MR. ROCHESTER WOULD BE **GLAD** IF **YOU** AND YOUR **PUPIL** WOULD TAKE **TEA** WITH HIM IN THE **DRAWING-ROOM** THIS EVENING.

WHAT **IS** HIS TEA-TIME?

AT **SIX O'CLOCK.** HE KEEPS **EARLY HOURS** IN THE **COUNTRY.**

N'EST-CE PAS, MONSIEUR, QU'IL Y A UN **CADEAU** POUR MADEMOISELLE EYRE DANS VOTRE **PETIT COFFRE?**

WHO TALKS OF **CADEAUX?** DID YOU EXPECT A **PRESENT,** MISS **EYRE?** ARE YOU **FOND** OF PRESENTS?

I HARDLY **KNOW,** SIR. I HAVE LITTLE **EXPERIENCE** OF THEM. THEY ARE **GENERALLY** THOUGHT **PLEASANT** THINGS.

GENERALLY **THOUGHT?** BUT WHAT DO **YOU** THINK?

A **PRESENT** HAS **MANY FACES** TO IT, AND ONE SHOULD CONSIDER **ALL,** BEFORE PRONOUNCING AN **OPINION** AS TO IT'S **NATURE.**

MISS **EYRE,** YOU ARE NOT SO **UNSOPHISTICATED** AS ADÈLE. SHE DEMANDS A "**CADEAU**" **CLAMOROUSLY,** THE **MOMENT** SHE **SEES** ME; **YOU** BEAT ABOUT THE **BUSH.**

BECAUSE I HAVE LESS **CONFIDENCE** IN MY **DESERTS** THAN ADÈLE HAS.

I AM A **STRANGER** AND HAVE DONE **NOTHING** TO ENTITLE ME TO AN **ACKNOWLEDGEMENT.**

OH, DON'T FALL BACK ON OVER-MODESTY! I HAVE EXAMINED ADÈLE, AND FIND YOU HAVE TAKEN GREAT PAINS WITH HER. SHE HAS NO TALENTS, YET IN A SHORT TIME SHE HAS MADE MUCH IMPROVEMENT.

SIR, YOU HAVE NOW GIVEN ME MY "CADEAU"; I AM OBLIGED TO YOU: IT IS THE MEED TEACHERS MOST COVET - PRAISE OF THEIR PUPILS' PROGRESS.

HUMPH!

YOU HAVE BEEN RESIDENT IN MY HOUSE THREE MONTHS NOW, AND YOU CAME FROM - ?

LOWOOD SCHOOL.

AH, A CHARITABLE CONCERN. HOW LONG WERE YOU THERE?

EIGHT YEARS, SIR.

EIGHT YEARS! YOU MUST BE TENACIOUS OF LIFE. I THOUGHT HALF THE TIME IN SUCH A PLACE WOULD HAVE DONE UP ANY CONSTITUTION!

NO WONDER YOU HAVE RATHER THE LOOK OF ANOTHER WORLD.

WHEN YOU CAME ON ME IN HAY LANE LAST NIGHT, I THOUGHT UNACCOUNTABLY OF FAIRY TALES, AND HAD HALF A MIND TO DEMAND WHETHER YOU HAD BEWITCHED MY HORSE.

WHO ARE YOUR PARENTS?

I HAVE NONE.

NOR EVER HAD, I SUPPOSE. DO YOU REMEMBER THEM?

NO.

I THOUGHT NOT. AND SO YOU WERE WAITING FOR YOUR PEOPLE WHEN YOU SAT ON THAT STILE?

FOR WHOM, SIR?

FOR THE MEN IN GREEN. IT WAS A PROPER MOONLIGHT EVENING FOR THEM. DID I BREAK THROUGH ONE OF YOUR RINGS, THAT YOU SPREAD THAT DAMNED ICE ON THE CAUSEWAY?

46

THE **MEN** IN **GREEN FORSOOK** ENGLAND A **HUNDRED YEARS** AGO, AND NOT EVEN IN **HAY LANE**, OR THE **FIELDS ABOUT** IT, COULD YOU FIND A **TRACE** OF THEM.

I DON'T THINK EITHER **SUMMER** OR **HARVEST**, OR **WINTER MOON**, WILL **EVER** SHINE ON THEIR **REVELS** MORE.

WELL, IF YOU DISOWN **PARENTS,** YOU MUST HAVE SOME SORT OF **KINSFOLK:** UNCLES AND **AUNTS?**

NO; NONE THAT I EVER **SAW;** AND NO **BROTHERS** OR **SISTERS**

WHO **RECOMMENDED** YOU TO COME **HERE?**

I **ADVERTISED,** AND MRS. FAIRFAX **ANSWERED.**

YES, AND I AM DAILY **THANKFUL** FOR THE CHOICE **PROVIDENCE** LED ME TO **MAKE.** MISS **EYRE** HAS BEEN AN **INVALUABLE COMPANION** TO ME, AND A **KIND** AND **CAREFUL** TEACHER TO **ADÈLE.**

DON'T **TROUBLE YOURSELF** TO GIVE HER A **CHARACTER.** I SHALL **JUDGE** FOR **MYSELF.**

SIR?

I HAVE TO **THANK HER** FOR THIS **SPRAIN.**

MISS **EYRE,** HAVE YOU EVER SEEN MUCH **SOCIETY?**

NONE BUT THE **PUPILS** AND **TEACHERS** OF **LOWOOD,** AND NOW THE **INMATES** OF **THORNFIELD.**

HAVE YOU **READ** MUCH?

ONLY SUCH **BOOKS** AS **CAME MY WAY,** AND THEY HAVE NOT BEEN **NUMEROUS,** OR VERY **LEARNED.**

YOU HAVE LIVED THE LIFE OF A **NUN:** NO **DOUBT** YOU ARE WELL **DRILLED** IN **RELIGIOUS** FORMS; BROCKLEHURST, WHO I UNDERSTAND **DIRECTS** LOWOOD, IS A **PARSON,** AND YOU **GIRLS** PROBABLY **WORSHIPPED** HIM, AS A **CONVENT** FULL OF **RELIGIEUSES** WOULD WORSHIP THEIR **DIRECTOR.**

47

OH, **NO.**

YOU'RE VERY **COOL.** - **NO!**

WHAT? A **NOVICE** NOT WORSHIP HER **PRIEST!** THAT SOUNDS **BLASPHEMOUS.**

I **DISLIKED** MR. BROCKLEHURST. HE IS A **HARSH MAN;** AT ONCE **POMPOUS** AND **MEDDLING;**

AND FOR **ECONOMY'S** SAKE BOUGHT US **BAD NEEDLES** AND **THREAD.**

THAT WAS VERY **FALSE ECONOMY.**

HE **STARVED** US BEFORE THE **COMMITTEE** WAS APPOINTED;

AND HE **BORED** US WITH LONG **LECTURES** ONCE A WEEK ABOUT **SUDDEN DEATHS** AND **JUDGMENTS,** WHICH MADE US **AFRAID** TO GO TO **BED.**

YOU STAYED THERE FOR **EIGHT YEARS:** YOU ARE NOW, THEN, **EIGHTEEN?**

YES, SIR.

IT IS A POINT **DIFFICULT** TO **FIX** WHERE THE **FEATURES** AND **COUNTENANCE** ARE SO MUCH AT **VARIANCE.**

CAN YOU **PLAY?**

A **LITTLE.**

SIT DOWN TO THE **PIANO** AND PLAY A **TUNE.**

ENOUGH!

YOU PLAY A **LITTLE,** I SEE; LIKE ANY **OTHER** ENGLISH SCHOOL-GIRL;

PERHAPS RATHER **BETTER** THAN SOME, BUT NOT **WELL.**

ADÈLE SHOWED ME SOME **SKETCHES** THIS MORNING, WHICH SHE SAID WERE **YOURS.**

I DON'T KNOW WHETHER THEY WERE **ENTIRELY** OF YOUR DOING; PROBABLY A **MASTER** AIDED YOU.

NO, INDEED!

AH! THAT PRICKS **PRIDE.**

WHERE DID YOU GET YOUR **COPIES?**

OUT OF MY **HEAD.**

HAS IT **OTHER** FURNITURE OF THE **SAME KIND** WITHIN?

I SHOULD **HOPE - BETTER.**

THESE **EYES,** YOU MUST HAVE SEEN IN A **DREAM.**

AND WHO TAUGHT YOU TO PAINT **WIND?** THERE IS A **HIGH GALE** IN THAT SKY, AND ON THIS **HILL-TOP.** WHERE DID YOU SEE **LATMOS?** FOR **THAT** IS **LATMOS.**

AND YOU FELT **SELF-SATISFIED** WITH THE RESULT OF YOUR **ARDENT LABOURS?**

FAR **FROM IT.** I WAS **TORMENTED** BY THE CONTRAST BETWEEN MY **IDEAS** AND MY **HANDIWORK.**

I HAD **IMAGINED** THINGS I WAS QUITE **POWERLESS** TO **REALISE.**

YOU HAD NOT ENOUGH OF THE ARTIST'S **SKILL** AND **SCIENCE** TO GIVE IT FULL **BEING,** YET THE DRAWINGS **ARE,** FOR A **SCHOOLGIRL,** PECULIAR.

AS TO THE **THOUGHTS,** THEY ARE **ELFISH.**

AT NINE O'CLOCK, I PUT ADÈLE TO **BED** AND JOINED **MRS. FAIRFAX** IN HER **ROOM.**

I FIND **MR. ROCHESTER** VERY **CHANGEFUL** AND **ABRUPT.**

TRUE: NO DOUBT HE MAY **APPEAR** SO TO A **STRANGER.**

BUT I AM SO **ACCUSTOMED** TO HIS MANNER, I NEVER **THINK** OF IT; AND THEN, IF HE HAS **PECULARITIES,** ALLOWANCE SHOULD BE MADE.

WHY?

FAMILY TROUBLES, FOR ONE THING. OUR MASTER **EDWARD** INHERITED **THORNFIELD** ONLY **NINE YEARS** AGO, AFTER HIS BROTHER **ROWLAND** DIED.

THEIR FATHER WAS **ANXIOUS** THAT MASTER **EDWARD** HAD **WEALTH TOO;** AND, SOON AFTER HE WAS **OF AGE,** SOME **STEPS** WERE TAKEN THAT PUT MASTER EDWARD IN A **PAINFUL POSITION.**

I DON'T THINK HE HAS EVER BEEN **RESIDENT** AT THORNFIELD FOR A **FORTNIGHT TOGETHER.**

49

CHAPTER XIV

SEVERAL **DAYS** PASSED WITH **LITTLE CONTACT** WITH **MR. ROCHESTER.**

MA BOÎTE! MA BOÎTE!

YES, THERE IS YOUR **"BOÎTE"** AT LAST. TAKE IT INTO A **CORNER,** YOU GENUINE DAUGHTER OF **PARIS,** AND AMUSE YOURSELF WITH DISEMBOWELLING IT. AND **MIND,** DON'T **BOTHER** ME WITH ANY **DETAILS** OF THE **ANATOMICAL PROCESS.** LET YOUR **OPERATION** BE CONDUCTED IN **SILENCE.** TIENS-TOI TRANQUILLE, ENFANT; COMPRENDS-TU?

COME **FORWARD,** MISS **EYRE; BE SEATED** HERE.

I AM NOT **FOND** OF THE **PRATTLE** OF **CHILDREN,** OLD **BACHELOR** AS I AM. IT WOULD BE **INTOLERABLE** TO ME TO PASS A **WHOLE EVENING** WITH A **BRAT.**

DON'T DRAW THAT CHAIR **FARTHER OFF,** MISS **EYRE.** SIT DOWN **EXACTLY** WHERE I **PLACED** IT - IF YOU **PLEASE,** THAT IS. **CONFOUND** THESE CIVILITIES! I CONTINUALLY **FORGET** THEM. NOR DO I **PARTICULARLY** AFFECT **SIMPLE-MINDED OLD LADIES...**

CHING! CHING!

*HE **RANG** AND DESPATCHED AN INVITATION TO MRS. FAIRFAX.*

GOOD **EVENING,** MADAM; I SENT TO YOU FOR A **CHARITABLE PURPOSE.** I HAVE **FORBIDDEN** ADÈLE TO TALK TO ME ABOUT HER **PRESENTS.**

HAVE THE **GOODNESS** TO SERVE HER AS **AUDITRESS** AND **INTERLOCUTRICE;** IT WILL BE ONE OF THE MOST **BENEVOLENT ACTS** YOU EVER **PERFORMED.**

NOW I HAVE PERFORMED THE PART OF A **GOOD HOST;** PUT MY **GUESTS** INTO THE WAY OF **AMUSING EACH OTHER.**

YOU **EXAMINE** ME, MISS EYRE. DO YOU THINK ME **HANDSOME?**

NO, SIR.

AH! BY MY **WORD!** THERE IS SOMETHING **SINGULAR** ABOUT YOU. YOU HAVE THE AIR OF A **LITTLE NONNETTE;** QUAINT, **QUIET, GRAVE** AND **SIMPLE;** AND **WHEN** ONE MAKES A **REMARK** TO WHICH YOU ARE **OBLIGED** TO **REPLY,** YOU RAP OUT A **ROUND REJOINDER,** WHICH, IF NOT BLUNT, IS AT LEAST **BRUSQUE.**

SIR, I WAS TOO PLAIN; I BEG YOUR PARDON. I OUGHT TO HAVE REPLIED THAT TASTES MOSTLY DIFFER, AND THAT BEAUTY IS OF LITTLE CONSEQUENCE, OR SOMETHING OF THAT SORT.

YOU OUGHT TO HAVE REPLIED NO SUCH THING.

BEAUTY OF LITTLE CONSEQUENCE, INDEED!

AND SO, UNDER PRETENCE OF SOFTENING THE PREVIOUS OUTRAGE, YOU STICK A SLY PENKNIFE UNDER MY EAR!

CRITICISE ME: DOES MY FOREHEAD NOT PLEASE YOU? AM I A FOOL?

FAR FROM IT, SIR. YOU WOULD, PERHAPS, THINK ME RUDE IF I INQUIRED WHETHER YOU ARE A PHILANTHROPIST?

THERE AGAIN! ANOTHER STICK OF THE PENKNIFE. NO, YOUNG LADY, I AM NOT A GENERAL PHILANTHROPIST, BUT I BEAR A CONSCIENCE.

FORTUNE HAS KNOCKED ME ABOUT, AND NOW I FLATTER MYSELF I AM HARD AND TOUGH AS AN INDIA-RUBBER BALL - THOUGH WITH ONE SENTIENT POINT IN THE MIDDLE OF THE LUMP.

DOES THAT LEAVE HOPE FOR ME?

HOPE OF WHAT, SIR?

OF MY FINAL RE-TRANSFORMATION FROM INDIA-RUBBER BACK TO FLESH?

YOU LOOK VERY MUCH PUZZLED, MISS EYRE:

AND THOUGH YOU ARE NOT PRETTY, ANY MORE THAN I AM HANDSOME, YET A PUZZLED AIR BECOMES YOU;

BESIDES, IT IS CONVENIENT, FOR IT KEEPS THOSE SEARCHING EYES OF YOURS AWAY FROM MY PHYSIOGNOMY, AND BUSIES THEM WITH THE WORSTED FLOWERS OF THE RUG; SO PUZZLE ON.

YOUNG **LADY**, I AM **DISPOSED** TO BE **GREGARIOUS** AND **COMMUNICATIVE** TONIGHT, AND THAT IS WHY I **SENT** FOR YOU. IT WOULD **PLEASE** ME NOW TO **DRAW YOU OUT** - TO LEARN **MORE** OF YOU - THEREFORE, **SPEAK**.

INSTEAD OF **SPEAKING**, I SMILED.

SPEAK.

WHAT **ABOUT**, SIR?

WHATEVER YOU **LIKE**.

I LEAVE THE CHOICE OF **SUBJECT** ENTIRELY TO **YOURSELF**.

IF HE EXPECTS ME TO **TALK** FOR THE MERE SAKE OF **TALKING** AND **SHOWING OFF**, HE WILL FIND HE HAS **ADDRESSED** HIMSELF TO THE **WRONG PERSON**.

YOU ARE **DUMB**, MISS EYRE. **STUBBORN** AND **ANNOYED**. AH! IT IS **CONSISTENT**.

MISS **EYRE**, I BEG YOUR **PARDON**. THE **FACT** IS, ONCE FOR **ALL**, I DON'T WISH TO **TREAT YOU** LIKE AN **INFERIOR**: THAT IS, I **CLAIM** ONLY SUCH **SUPERIORITY** AS MUST RESULT FROM **TWENTY YEARS'** DIFFERENCE IN **AGE** AND A **CENTURY'S** ADVANCE IN **EXPERIENCE**.

HE HAD DESIGNED AN **EXPLANATION**; ALMOST AN **APOLOGY**.

DO YOU **AGREE** THAT I HAVE A **RIGHT** TO BE **MASTERFUL**, **ABRUPT**, PERHAPS **EXACTING**, SOMETIMES?

DO AS YOU **PLEASE**, SIR.

THAT IS **NO ANSWER**; OR RATHER IT IS A VERY **IRRITATING**, BECAUSE A VERY **EVASIVE**, ONE.

REPLY **CLEARLY**.

I DON'T **THINK**, SIR, YOU HAVE A RIGHT TO COMMAND ME, MERELY BECAUSE YOU ARE **OLDER** THAN I, OR BECAUSE YOU HAVE SEEN **MORE** OF THE WORLD THAN I HAVE; YOUR CLAIM TO **SUPERIORITY** DEPENDS ON THE **USE** YOU HAVE MADE OF YOUR **TIME** AND **EXPERIENCE**.

HUMPH! PROMPTLY SPOKEN.

BUT I WON'T ALLOW THAT AS I HAVE MADE AN INDIFFERENT USE OF BOTH ADVANTAGES.

LEAVING SUPERIORITY OUT OF THE QUESTION, THEN, YOU MUST STILL AGREE TO RECEIVE MY ORDERS NOW AND THEN, WITHOUT BEING PIQUED OR HURT BY THE TONE OF COMMAND. WILL YOU?

HE SEEMS TO FORGET THAT HE PAYS ME THIRTY POUNDS PER ANNUM FOR RECEIVING HIS ORDERS.

THE SMILE IS VERY WELL, BUT SPEAK, TOO.

I WAS THINKING THAT VERY FEW MASTERS WOULD TROUBLE THEMSELVES TO INQUIRE WHETHER OR NOT THEIR PAID SUBORDINATES WERE PIQUED AND HURT BY THEIR ORDERS.

PAID SUBORDINATES! WHAT! YOU ARE MY PAID SUBORDINATE, ARE YOU?

OH YES, I HAD FORGOTTEN THE SALARY! WELL, THEN, ON THAT MERCENARY GROUND, WILL YOU AGREE TO LET ME HECTOR A LITTLE?

NO, SIR, NOT ON THAT GROUND; BUT ON THE GROUND THAT YOU DID FORGET IT, AND THAT YOU CARE WHETHER OR NOT A DEPENDENT IS COMFORTABLE IN HIS DEPENDENCY, I AGREE HEARTILY.

AND WILL YOU CONSENT TO DISPENSE WITH A GREAT MANY CONVENTIONAL FORMS AND PHRASES, WITHOUT THINKING THAT THE OMISSION ARISES FROM INSOLENCE?

53

I AM **SURE**, SIR, I SHOULD NEVER MISTAKE **INFORMALITY** FOR **INSOLENCE**: ONE I RATHER **LIKE**, THE **OTHER** NOTHING **FREE-BORN** WOULD **SUBMIT** TO, EVEN **FOR A SALARY**.

HUMBUG! MOST THINGS **FREE-BORN** WILL SUBMIT TO **ANYTHING** FOR A **SALARY**.

HOWEVER, I MENTALLY **SHAKE HANDS** WITH YOU FOR YOUR ANSWER, **DESPITE** IT'S INACCURACY.

NOT **THREE** IN **THREE THOUSAND** RAW **SCHOOLGIRL-GOVERNESSES** WOULD HAVE ANSWERED ME AS **YOU** HAVE JUST DONE.

BUT I DON'T MEAN TO **FLATTER** YOU: IT IS NO MERIT OF **YOURS**. **NATURE** DID IT.

FOR WHAT I **YET** KNOW, YOU MAY HAVE **INTOLERABLE DEFECTS** TO COUNTERBALANCE YOUR FEW **GOOD POINTS**.

AND SO MAY **YOU**.

I HAVE **PLENTY** OF FAULTS OF MY **OWN**. I **MIGHT** HAVE BEEN AS GOOD AS **YOU**. NATURE **MEANT** ME TO BE, ON THE **WHOLE**, A **GOOD MAN**, MISS **EYRE**; AND YOU **SEE** I AM **NOT SO**.

WHEN FATE **WRONGED** ME, I HAD NOT THE **WISDOM** TO STAY **COOL**. DREAD **REMORSE**, MISS **EYRE**; REMORSE IS THE **POISON** OF **LIFE**.

REPENTANCE IS SAID TO BE ITS **CURE**, SIR.

IT IS **NOT** ITS **CURE**. **REFORMATION** MAY BE ITS CURE.

ting ting ting

I SEE YOU LAUGH **RARELY** AND YOU **FEAR** TO **SMILE**: BUT, IN **TIME**, I THINK YOU WILL LEARN TO BE **NATURAL** WITH ME, AS I FIND IT **IMPOSSIBLE** TO BE **CONVENTIONAL** WITH **YOU**.

IT HAS STRUCK **NINE**, SIR. IT IS **ADÈLE'S BEDTIME**.

ting ting ting ting ting

NEVER **MIND** - WAIT A **MINUTE**: ADÈLE IS NOT **READY** TO GO TO BED **YET**.

SHE PULLED OUT OF HER **BOX**, ABOUT **TEN MINUTES** AGO, A LITTLE PINK **FROCK**; **RAPTURE** LIT HER **FACE** AS SHE **UNFOLDED** IT. SHE IS NOW WITH **SOPHIE**, UNDERGOING A **ROBING PROCESS**.

IN A FEW **MINUTES** SHE WILL **RE-ENTER**, AND I **KNOW** WHAT I SHALL **SEE** - A **MINIATURE** OF **CÉLINE VARENS**, AS SHE USED TO APPEAR ON THE **BOARDS** AT THE **RISING OF** --

-- BUT NEVER MIND **THAT**

STAY NOW, TO SEE WHETHER IT WILL BE **REALISED**.

MONSIEUR, JE VOUS REMERCIE MILLE FOIS DE VOTRE **BONTÉ**. C'EST COMME CELA QUE **MAMA FAISAIT**, N'EST-CE PAS, MONSIEUR?

PRE-CISE-LY! AND, '**COMME CELA**', SHE CHARMED MY **ENGLISH GOLD** OUT OF MY **BRITISH BREECHES'** POCKET.

I HAVE BEEN **GREEN**, TOO, **MISS EYRE** - AY, **GRASS GREEN**. MY **SPRING** IS GONE, BUT IT HAS **LEFT** ME THAT **FRENCH FLOWERET** ON MY HANDS, WHICH IN SOME MOODS, I WOULD BE **FAIN** BE RID OF. I **KEEP** IT AND **REAR** IT RATHER ON THE ROMAN CATHOLIC PRINCIPLE OF EXPIATING NUMEROUS SINS BY **ONE GOOD WORK**.

I'LL **EXPLAIN** ALL THIS SOME DAY.

MR. ROCHESTER *DID*, ON A *FUTURE* OCCASION, *EXPLAIN* IT.

ADÈLE WAS THE DAUGHTER OF A FRENCH OPERA-DANCER, *CÉLINE VARENS*, FOR WHOM I ONCE CHERISHED A *'GRANDE PASSION'*.

THIS *PASSION* CÉLINE PROFESSED TO *RETURN* WITH EVEN *SUPERIOR ARDOUR*.

AND, MISS *EYRE*, SO *MUCH* WAS I *FLATTERED* BY THIS *PREFERENCE* OF THE *GALLIC SYLPH* FOR HER *BRITISH GNOME*, THAT I *INSTALLED* HER IN AN *HOTEL*; GAVE HER A COMPLETE *ESTABLISHMENT* OF *SERVANTS*; A *CARRIAGE*, *DIAMONDS* --

~ CHAPTER XV ~

-- IN *SHORT*, I BEGAN THE *PROCESS* OF *RUINING MYSELF*.

HAPPENING TO *CALL* ONE EVENING WHEN *CÉLINE* DID NOT *EXPECT* ME, I FOUND HER *OUT*.

THE *BALCONY* WAS FURNISHED WITH A *CHAIR* OR TWO, AND I SAT THERE IN THE *WARM EVENING*.

THE *VOITURE* I HAD GIVEN HER ARRIVED AND MY FLAME *ALIGHTED* - I WAS ABOUT TO *CALL* HER WHEN A *FIGURE* JUMPED FROM THE CARRIAGE *AFTER* HER.

YOU NEVER FELT *JEALOUSY*, DID YOU, MISS *EYRE*?

OF *COURSE* NOT. BECAUSE YOU NEVER FELT *LOVE*.

BUT I *TELL* YOU, YOU WILL *COME* SOME DAY TO A *CRAGGY PASS*: EITHER YOU WILL BE *DASHED* TO *ATOMS*, OR *LIFTED UP* INTO A *CALMER* CURRENT - AS *I AM* NOW.

I *LIKE* THIS DAY. I LIKE THAT *SKY OF STEEL*.

I LIKE *THORNFIELD*; ITS GREY *FAÇADE*; AND YET HOW *LONG* HAVE I *SHUNNED* IT LIKE A GREAT *PLAGUE-HOUSE*?

HOW I DO STILL *ABHOR*...

HE GROUND HIS *TEETH* AND WAS SILENT. SOME *HATED* THOUGHT SEEMED TO HAVE HIM IN ITS *GRIP*.

DURING THE MOMENT I WAS **SILENT**, MISS **EYRE**, I WAS ARRANGING A **POINT** WITH MY **DESTINY**. SHE **STOOD** THERE, A **HAG** LIKE ONE OF THOSE WHO APPEARED TO **MACBETH**.

"YOU LIKE **THORNFIELD?**" SHE SAID AND **WROTE** IN THE **AIR** ALL ALONG THE **HOUSE-FRONT:**

"**LIKE IT IF YOU CAN! LIKE IT IF YOU DARE!**"

"I **WILL** LIKE IT", SAID I. "I **DARE** LIKE IT".

I WILL **BREAK** OBSTACLES TO **HAPPINESS**, TO **GOODNESS** – YES, **GOODNESS**.

DID YOU **LEAVE** THE **BALCONY**, SIR, WHEN MADEMOISELLE VARENS ENTERED?

OH, I HAD FORGOTTEN CÉLINE! **WELL**, TO **RESUME**, I REMAINED IN THE **BALCONY** AND DREW THE **CURTAIN**.

THE PAIR CAME **IN**, AND REMOVED THEIR **CLOAKS**. THERE WAS "THE VARENS" SHINING IN **SATIN** AND **JEWELS** – MY GIFTS OF COURSE – AND THERE WAS HER **COMPANION** IN AN **OFFICER'S** UNIFORM. I **KNEW** HIM – A **BRAINLESS, VICIOUS** YOUTH WHOM I **DESPISED**. OPENING THE **WINDOW**, I **WALKED IN** UPON THEM; **LIBERATED** CÉLINE FROM MY PROTECTION, DISREGARDED **SCREAMS** AND **HYSTERICS** AND MADE AN **APPOINTMENT** WITH THE **VICOMTE** FOR A **MEETING** AT THE **BOIS DE BOULOGNE**.

NEXT **MORNING** I HAD THE PLEASURE OF LEAVING A **BULLET** IN ONE OF HIS POOR ETIOLATED **ARMS**, **FEEBLE** AS THE WING OF A **CHICKEN**.

I **THOUGHT** I HAD **DONE** WITH THE **WHOLE CREW**. BUT **UNLUCKILY** THE VARENS, SIX MONTHS BEFORE, HAD GIVEN ME THIS **FILETTE**, **ADÈLE**, WHO, SHE AFFIRMED, WAS MY **DAUGHTER**.

PERHAPS SHE MAY BE, THOUGH I SEE NO **PROOFS** OF SUCH **GRIM** PATERNITY WRITTEN IN HER **COUNTENANCE**. HER MOTHER **ABANDONED** HER CHILD AND **RAN AWAY** TO ITALY.

I ACKNOWLEDGED NO **NATURAL CLAIM**, FOR I AM **NOT** HER **FATHER;** BUT HEARING THAT SHE WAS **DESTITUTE**, I **TRANSPLANTED** HER HERE.

NOW YOU **KNOW**, YOU WILL PERHAPS **BEG** ME TO LOOK OUT FOR A **NEW** GOVERNESS, EH?

NO: ADÈLE IS NOT **ANSWERABLE** FOR EITHER HER **MOTHER'S** FAULTS OR **YOURS**.

FORSAKEN BY HER **MOTHER** AND **DISOWNED** BY **YOU**, SIR – I SHALL **CLING CLOSER** TO HER THAN **BEFORE**.

I COULD NOT **SLEEP** FOR THINKING OF HIS **LOOK** WHEN HE TOLD HOW HIS **DESTINY** HAD **RISEN UP** BEFORE HIM.

I HARDLY KNOW WHETHER I HAD **SLEPT** OR **NOT** AFTER THIS MUSING WHEN I HEARD A **SOUND...**

EEE-EEE-AH-HA...

WHO IS THERE?

WAS THAT **GRACE POOLE?** AND IS SHE **POSSESSED** WITH A **DEVIL?**

THUD
THUD
THUD
THUD
CREAK
CLUNK

I THOUGHT AT **FIRST** THE GOBLIN LAUGHTER STOOD AT MY **BEDSIDE.** ERE **LONG,** STEPS RETREATED TOWARDS THE THIRD-STORY **STAIRCASE:** A DOOR **OPENED** AND **CLOSED,** AND ALL WAS **STILL.**

!

WAKE! WAKE!

HISSSSSS

58

IS THERE A **FLOOD**?

NO, SIR. BUT THERE **HAS** BEEN A **FIRE**.

IN THE NAME OF **ALL** THE **ELVES** IN **CHRISTENDOM**, IS THAT **JANE EYRE**? HAVE YOU PLOTTED TO **DROWN** ME?

SOMEBODY HAS **PLOTTED SOMETHING**.

YOU CANNOT **TOO SOON** FIND OUT **WHO** AND **WHAT** IT WAS.

I BRIEFLY **RELATED** TO HIM WHAT HAD **TRANSPIRED**. HE LISTENED VERY **GRAVELY**; HIS **FACE** EXPRESSED MORE **CONCERN** THAN **ASTONISHMENT**.

REMAIN WHERE YOU **ARE**; BE AS **STILL** AS A **MOUSE**.

DON'T **MOVE**, REMEMBER, OR CALL ANYONE.

A **VERY LONG TIME** ELAPSED...

I HAVE **FOUND IT ALL OUT**. I **FORGET** WHETHER YOU SAID YOU **SAW** ANYTHING WHEN YOU **OPENED** YOUR **CHAMBER DOOR**.

ONLY THE **CANDLESTICK**.

BUT YOU HEARD AN **ODD LAUGH**?

YES, SIR: A **WOMAN** WHO **SEWS** HERE, CALLED **GRACE POOLE** - SHE LAUGHS THAT WAY.

JUST **SO**. **GRACE POOLE** - YOU HAVE **GUESSED** IT. SAY NOTHING ABOUT TO-NIGHT'S **INCIDENT**.

YOU HAVE **SAVED** MY **LIFE**. I HAVE A **PLEASURE** IN **OWING** YOU SO **IMMENSE** A **DEBT**.

GOOD-NIGHT, SIR.

THERE IS NO **DEBT, BENEFIT, OBLIGATION** IN THE **CASE**.

I **KNEW** YOU WOULD DO ME **GOOD** IN SOME WAY, AT **SOME** TIME.

MY **CHERISHED PRESERVER, GOOD-NIGHT!**

I AM **GLAD** I HAPPENED TO BE **AWAKE**.

I **THINK** I HEAR **MRS. FAIRFAX** MOVE, SIR.

WELL, LEAVE ME.

I REGAINED MY **COUCH**, BUT NEVER THOUGHT OF **SLEEP**. TOO **FEVERISH** TO REST, I **ROSE** AS SOON AS **DAY DAWNED**.

THE NEXT **MORNING**, I WAS **AMAZED** TO FIND **GRACE POOLE** SEWING **RINGS** TO NEW **CURTAINS** IN **MR. ROCHESTER'S** BEDROOM. THERE WAS **NO SIGN** OF **DESPERATION** FROM THE **WOMAN** WHO HAD ATTEMPTED **MURDER**.

~ CHAPTER XVI ~

MASTER HAD BEEN **READING** IN HIS **BED** LAST NIGHT;

HE FELL **ASLEEP** WITH HIS **CANDLE** LIT, AND THE **CURTAINS** GOT ON **FIRE**.

DID **MR. ROCHESTER** WAKE NOBODY?

THE **SERVANTS** SLEEP **TOO FAR AWAY**. **YOU'RE** NEAREST; PERHAPS **YOU** MAY HAVE HEARD A NOISE?

I AM **CERTAIN** I HEARD A **LAUGH**, AND A **STRANGE** ONE.

IT IS HARDLY **LIKELY** MASTER WOULD **LAUGH**, WHEN HE WAS IN SUCH **DANGER**: YOU MUST HAVE BEEN **DREAMING**.

I WAS **NOT** DREAMING.

I HAD **SO MANY THINGS** TO SAY TO **MR. ROCHESTER**! I WANTED **AGAIN** TO INTRODUCE THE SUBJECT OF **GRACE POOLE**, AND TO **HEAR** WHAT HE WOULD **ANSWER**; BUT I DIDN'T **HEAR HIM** IN THE **HOUSE**.

DIRECTLY AFTER **BREAKFAST**, **MR. ROCHESTER** SET OFF FOR **THE LEAS**, MR. **ESHTON'S** PLACE. THERE IS **QUITE** A **PARTY** THERE, AND IS **LIKELY** TO STAY A **WEEK** OR MORE.

ARE THERE **LADIES** AT **THE LEAS?**

THERE ARE **MRS. ESHTON** AND HER **THREE DAUGHTERS**; AND THERE ARE **BLANCHE** AND **MARY INGRAM**, I SUPPOSE.

BLANCHE WAS THE **BELLE** OF A **CHRISTMAS BALL** MR. **ROCHESTER** GAVE AROUND **SEVEN YEARS AGO**.

THEY **SANG** A **DUET**...

I WAS NOT **AWARE** THAT **MR. ROCHESTER** COULD SING.

HE HAS A **FINE BASS VOICE**.

AND **MISS INGRAM**?

A **VERY RICH** ONE.

I **WONDER** NO **WEALTHY GENTLEMAN** HAS TAKEN A **FANCY** TO HER: **MR. ROCHESTER**, FOR INSTANCE.

HE IS NEARLY **FORTY**; **SHE** IS BUT **TWENTY-FIVE**.

WHEN ONCE MORE **ALONE**, I **REVIEWED** THE INFORMATION I HAD GOT. A **GREATER FOOL** THAN **JANE EYRE** HAD **NEVER** BREATHED THE **BREATH** OF **LIFE**.

YOU, A **FAVOURITE** OF **MR. ROCHESTER**? **GO!** YOUR **FOLLY SICKENS** ME. **POOR STUPID DOPE!**

I **SENTENCED** MYSELF TO **DRAW** MY **OWN PICTURE**; WITHOUT **SOFTENING** ONE **DEFECT**...

PORTRAIT of a GOVERNESS DISCONNECTED – POOR, AND PLAIN.

...AND **THEN**, WITH MY **FINEST**, **CLEAREST TINTS**, TO PAINT THE **LOVELIEST FACE** I COULD **IMAGINE**, AND CALL IT '**BLANCHE, AN ACCOMPLISHED LADY OF RANK**'.

I DERIVED **BENEFIT** FROM THE TASK: IT HAD KEPT MY **HEAD** AND **HANDS** EMPLOYED. ERE **LONG**, I HAD REASON TO **CONGRATULATE** MYSELF ON THE COURSE OF **WHOLESOME DISCIPLINE** TO WHICH I HAD **THUS** FORCED MY **FEELINGS** TO **SUBMIT**.

~ CHAPTER XVII ~

MR. ROCHESTER HAD BEEN **ABSENT** UPWARDS OF A **FORTNIGHT**, WHEN THE **POST** BROUGHT **MRS. FAIRFAX** A **LETTER**.

MR. ROCHESTER IS NOT LIKELY TO **RETURN** SOON, I **SUPPOSE**?

INDEED HE **IS** – IN **THREE** DAYS; AND NOT **ALONE** EITHER.

HE SENDS **DIRECTIONS** FOR ALL THE **BEST BEDROOMS** TO BE PREPARED; AND **ROOMS** TO BE **CLEANED OUT**.

THE THREE DAYS WERE **BUSY** ENOUGH. THREE WOMEN WERE GOT TO **HELP**. **ADÈLE** RAN **QUITE WILD** IN THE **MIDST** OF IT: THE **PREPARATIONS** AND THE PROSPECT OF **COMPANY** SEEMED TO THROW HER INTO **ECSTASIES**.

MRS. FAIRFAX HAD **PRESSED** ME INTO HER **SERVICE**, AND I WAS **ALL DAY** HELPING (OR **HINDERING**) HER AND THE **COOK**.

GRACE POOLE SPENT **MOST** OF THE TIME IN SOME **CHAMBER** OF THE **THIRD STORY**: THERE SHE **SAT** AND **SEWED**...

...AS **COMPANIONLESS** AS A **PRISONER** IN HIS **DUNGEON**.

THE **DAY CAME**: ALL **WORK** HAD BEEN **COMPLETED** THE **PREVIOUS** EVENING.

IT GETS **LATE**.

I AM GLAD I ORDERED **DINNER** AN **HOUR AFTER** THE TIME MR. **ROCHESTER** MENTIONED.

MISS INGRAM!

THE FOLLOWING *EVENING,* MR. ROCHESTER INSISTED THAT I *ACCOMPANY* ADÈLE TO THE DRAWING-ROOM AFTER *DINNER.*

A *BAND* OF LADIES ENTERED AND THE *CURTAIN* FELL *BEHIND* THEM.

BON JOUR, MESDAMES.

OH, WHAT A LITTLE *PUPPET!*

IT IS MR. ROCHESTER'S WARD, I SUPPOSE - THE *LITTLE* FRENCH GIRL HE WAS SPEAKING OF.

WHAT A *LOVE* OF A *CHILD!*

63

AT LAST *COFFEE* IS BROUGHT IN, AND THE *GENTLEMEN* ARE SUMMONED. I SIT IN THE *SHADE*; THE *WINDOW-CURTAIN* HALF *HIDES* ME.

AND *WHERE* IS MR. *ROCHESTER?*

HE COMES IN *LAST*: I AM NOT *LOOKING*, YET I *SEE HIM* ENTER.

CONVERSATION WAXES *BRISK* AND *MERRY*. *HENRY*, THE SON OF *LADY LYNN* IS TRYING TO TALK *FRENCH* WITH *ADÈLE*, AND *LOUISA ESHTON* LAUGHS AT HIS *BLUNDERS*.

THE TWO PROUD *DOWAGERS*, LADY *LYNN* AND LADY *INGRAM*, *CONFABULATE* TOGETHER;

SIR GEORGE OCCASIONALLY PUTS IN A *WORD*.

COLONEL *DENT* AND MR. *ESHTON* ARGUE ABOUT *POLITICS*; THEIR *WIVES* LISTEN.

LORD *INGRAM* LEANS ON THE *CHAIR-BACK* OF *AMY ESHTON*;

SHE LIKES *HIM* BETTER THAN SHE DOES MR. *ROCHESTER*.

I COMPARED *MR. ROCHESTER* WITH HIS *GUESTS*. I SAW THEM *SMILE*, *LAUGH* - IT WAS *NOTHING*; I SAW *MR. ROCHESTER* SMILE - HIS *STERN* FEATURES *SOFTENED*.

HE IS NOT TO *THEM* WHAT HE IS TO *ME*.

I MUST *REMEMBER* THAT HE CANNOT *CARE* MUCH FOR ME - AND *YET*, WHILE I *BREATHE* AND *THINK*, I MUST LOVE HIM.

WHENEVER I MARRY, I AM **RESOLVED** MY HUSBAND SHALL NOT BE A **RIVAL**, BUT A **FOIL** TO ME. I SHALL **SUFFER** NO **COMPETITOR** NEAR THE **THRONE**.

MR. ROCHESTER, NOW **SING**, AND I WILL **PLAY** FOR YOU.

I AM ALL **OBEDIENCE**.

NOW IS MY **TIME** TO **SLIP AWAY**.

BUT THE **TONES** THAT THEN **SEVERED** THE **AIR ARRESTED** ME.

I **WAITED** TILL THE **LAST DEEP** AND **FULL VIBRATION** OF MR. ROCHESTER'S FINE **VOICE** HAD **EXPIRED** AND MADE MY **EXIT**.

UTSIDE, I STOPPED TO TIE MY SANDAL...

WHY DID YOU NOT COME AND **SPEAK** TO ME IN THE **ROOM**?

YOU SEEMED **ENGAGED**, SIR.

YOU ARE **DESERTING** TOO **EARLY**.

I AM **TIRED**, SIR.

AND A LITTLE **DEPRESSED**. WHAT ABOUT?

NOTHING, SIR. I AM NOT **DEPRESSED**.

BUT I **AFFIRM** THAT YOU **ARE** - SO MUCH DEPRESSED THAT A **FEW MORE WORDS** WOULD BRING **TEARS** TO YOUR **EYES**.

WELL, **TO-NIGHT** I **EXCUSE** YOU; BUT WHILE MY **VISITORS** STAY, I **EXPECT** YOU TO APPEAR IN THE **DRAWING-ROOM** EVERY **EVENING**.

IT IS MY **WISH**.

GOODNIGHT, MY --

HE **STOPPED**, BIT HIS **LIP**, AND **ABRUPTLY** LEFT ME.

MERRY DAYS WERE *THESE* AT *THORNFIELD HALL.* ALL *SAD FEELINGS* SEEMED NOW *DRIVEN* FROM THE *HOUSE.* EVEN WHEN *RAIN* SET IN, INDOOR *AMUSEMENTS* BECAME MORE *LIVELY,* LIKE *'CHARADES'.*

~ CHAPTER XVIII ~

BRIDEWELL!

I HAD *LEARNT* TO *LOVE* MR. ROCHESTER. I COULD NOT *UN-LOVE* HIM NOW, *MERELY* BECAUSE HE HAD *CEASED* TO *NOTICE* ME. I SAW *ALL* HIS ATTENTIONS *APPROPRIATED* BY MISS INGRAM.

VOILÀ, MONSIEUR ROCHESTER!

IT IS *NOT* MR. ROCHESTER, YOU *TIRESOME MONKEY!*

I WAS NOT *JEALOUS:* SHE WAS TOO *INFERIOR* TO *EXCITE* THE *FEELING.* SHE WAS VERY *SHOWY,* BUT SHE WAS NOT *GENUINE.* SHE COULD NOT *CHARM* HIM.

SOON, THE *NEW-COMER* ENTERED. HIS *MANNER* WAS *POLITE,* AND HE WAS A *FINE-LOOKING* MAN, AT *FIRST SIGHT* ESPECIALLY.

IT *APPEARS* I COME AT AN *INOPPORTUNE TIME,* MADAM, WHEN MY *FRIEND,* MR. ROCHESTER, IS *FROM HOME;*

BUT I *ARRIVE* FROM THE *WEST INDIES,* AND I *THINK* I MAY *PRESUME* TO *INSTALL MYSELF* HERE TILL HE *RETURNS.*

I *PRESENTLY* GATHERED THAT THE *NEW-COMER* WAS CALLED *MR. MASON.*

AFTER DINNER...

LADIES, **SAM**, HERE SAYS THAT A GIPSY IS IN THE **SERVANTS' HALL**, AND INSISTS UPON TELLING OUR **FORTUNES**.

DISMISS HER, BY **ALL MEANS**, AT **ONCE**!

BUT WE **CANNOT** PERSUADE HER TO GO AWAY, MY **LADY**.

SHE **SWEARS** SHE MUST **TELL** THE **GENTRY** THEIR **FORTUNES**.
SHE'LL HAVE **NO** GENTLEMEN, NOR ANY **LADIES**, EXCEPT THE **YOUNG** AND **SINGLE**.

TELL HER SHE SHALL BE **PUT** IN THE **STOCKS** IF SHE **DOESN'T LEAVE**.

I CANNOT **POSSIBLY** COUNTENANCE THIS.

INDEED, MAMA, BUT YOU **CAN** AND **WILL**.
I HAVE A **CURIOSITY** TO **HEAR** MY **FORTUNE** TOLD. I GO **FIRST**.

FIFTEEN MINUTES **LATER...**

WELL, BLANCHE?

I HAVE **SEEN** A GIPSY VAGABOND.

SHE HAS **TOLD** ME WHAT **SUCH** PEOPLE **USUALLY** TELL.

MY **WHIM** IS **GRATIFIED**; AND **NOW** I THINK MR. **ESHTON** WILL DO WELL TO PUT THE **HAG** IN THE **STOCKS** TO-MORROW MORNING, AS HE **THREATENED**.

NEXT, **MARY INGRAM, AMY** AND **LOUISA ESHTON** WENT **TOGETHER** AND **RETURNED** HALF-SCARED OUT OF THEIR **WITS**.

IF YOU **PLEASE**, MISS, THE **GIPSY** DECLARES THAT THERE IS **ANOTHER** YOUNG SINGLE LADY IN THE ROOM WHO HAS **NOT BEEN** TO HER YET.
I **THOUGHT** IT MUST BE **YOU**. WHAT SHALL I **TELL** HER?

OH, I WILL **GO** BY **ALL MEANS**. I AM **NOT** IN THE **LEAST** AFRAID.

67

THERE WAS *NOTHING INDEED* IN THE GIPSY'S *APPEARANCE* TO *TROUBLE* ONE'S *CALM*. WE WERE *SOON* DISCUSSING MR. *ROCHESTER...*

IS IT *KNOWN* THAT MR. *ROCHESTER* IS TO BE *MARRIED?*

YES; AND TO THE *BEAUTIFUL* MISS *INGRAM.*

HE *MUST* LOVE SUCH A *HANDSOME, NOBLE, WITTY, ACCOMPLISHED* LADY; AND *PROBABLY* SHE LOVES *HIM,* OR, IF NOT HIS *PERSON,* AT LEAST HIS *PURSE.*

THOUGH - GOD *PARDON* ME! - I *TOLD* HER SOMETHING ON *THAT* POINT WHICH MADE HER LOOK *WONDROUS GRAVE.*

~ CHAPTER XIX ~

SUDDENLY I SAW A *BROAD RING* WITH A *GEM* I HAD SEEN A *HUNDRED TIMES BEFORE.* THE *BONNET* WAS *DOFFED,* AND THE *HEAD* ADVANCED.

DO YOU *FORGIVE* ME, *JANE?*

I SHALL *TRY* TO FORGIVE YOU; BUT IT WAS *NOT RIGHT.*

I HAVE *PERMISSION* TO RETIRE NOW, I *SUPPOSE?*

NO; STAY A MOMENT; AND *TELL* ME WHAT THE PEOPLE IN THE *DRAWING-ROOM* ARE DOING.

DISCUSSING THE *GIPSY,* I *DARESAY.*

OH, ARE YOU *AWARE* THAT A *STRANGER* ARRIVED HERE?

DID HE GIVE HIS *NAME?*

MASON.

MASON!

-- FROM THE *WEST INDIES!*

DO YOU FEEL *ILL,* SIR? OH, *LEAN* ON ME, SIR.

MY LITTLE *FRIEND,* I WISH I WERE IN A *QUIET ISLAND* WITH *ONLY YOU;*

AND *TROUBLE,* AND *DANGER* AND *HIDEOUS* RECOLLECTIONS *REMOVED* FROM ME.

~ CHAPTER XX ~

THAT NIGHT...

ARRRGHH!!
EEIIIGHH!!

GOOD GOD!
WHAT A CRY!

IT CAME OUT OF THE THIRD STORY; FOR IT PASSED OVERHEAD.

I NOW HEARD A STRUGGLE: A DEADLY ONE IT SEEMED FROM THE NOISE.

HELP! HELP! HELP!

ROCHESTER!

FOR GOD'S SAKE, COME!

WHAT AWFUL EVENT HAS TAKEN PLACE?

A SERVANT HAS HAD THE NIGHTMARE; THAT IS ALL.

NOW I MUST SEE YOU ALL BACK INTO YOUR ROOMS; FOR, TILL THE HOUSE IS SETTLED, SHE CANNOT BE LOOKED AFTER.

HE CONTRIVED TO GET THEM ALL ONCE MORE ENCLOSED IN THEIR SEPARATE DORMITORIES. I, ON THE CONTRARY, BEGAN AND DRESSED MYSELF CAREFULLY, TO BE READY FOR EMERGENCIES.

STILLNESS RETURNED; AND IN ABOUT AN HOUR THORNFIELD HALL WAS AGAIN AS HUSHED AS THE DESERT.

A CAUTIOUS HAND TAPPED LOW AT THE DOOR.

I want you.
Come this way and make no noise.
Bring a sponge and any volatile salts you may have.

GRR-RR, RUGG-LL, HAHA!

YOU DON'T TURN SICK AT THE SIGHT OF BLOOD?

I THINK I SHALL NOT. I HAVE NEVER BEEN TRIED YET.

GIVE ME YOUR HAND.

IT WILL NOT DO TO RISK A FAINTING FIT.

MR. MASON!

JANE, I SHALL HAVE TO **LEAVE YOU** IN **HERE** WHILE I FETCH A **SURGEON**.

SPONGE THE **BLOOD;** IF HE FEELS **FAINT,** YOU WILL PUT THE **GLASS OF WATER** TO HIS **LIPS** AND YOUR **SALTS** TO HIS **NOSE.**

IS THERE **IMMEDIATE DANGER?**

POOH! NO - A MERE **SCRATCH.** BEAR UP, MAN!

JANE, DO NOT **SPEAK** TO HIM ON **ANY PRETEXT**

- AND -

RICHARD, IT WILL BE AT THE **PERIL** OF YOUR **LIFE** IF **YOU SPEAK** TO HER. IF YOU **DO,** I'LL NOT **ANSWER** FOR THE **CONSEQUENCES.**

TWO HOURS **LATER,** MR. **ROCHESTER** RETURNED WITH THE **SURGEON.**

SHE'S **DONE** FOR ME, I **FEAR!** ROCHESTER GOT THE **KNIFE** FROM HER.

THERE HAVE BEEN **TEETH** HERE!

SHE **SUCKED** THE **BLOOD:** SHE **SAID** SHE'D **DRAIN** MY **HEART.**

NEVER MIND HER **GIBBERISH:** DON'T **REPEAT** IT.

HURRY!

I MUST HAVE HIM **OFF** BEFORE **SUNRISE.**

AT HALF-PAST **FIVE,** MR. **MASON** WAS **ASSISTED** INTO THE **CHAISE.**

LET HER BE **TAKEN CARE OF:** LET HER BE **TREATED** AS **TENDERLY** AS **MAY BE;** LET HER -

sob *sob*

I DO MY **BEST;** AND **HAVE** DONE IT, AND **WILL** DO IT.

70

YET **WOULD** TO **GOD** THERE WAS AN **END** OF ALL THIS!

JANE! **COME** WHERE THERE IS SOME **FRESHNESS.** THAT **HOUSE** IS A MERE **DUNGEON:** DON'T YOU **FEEL** IT SO?

IT **SEEMS** TO **ME** A **SPLENDID MANSION,** SIR.

THE **GLAMOUR** OF **INEXPERIENCE** IS OVER YOUR **EYES.** YOU CANNOT **DISCERN** THAT THE **GILDING** IS **SLIME** AND THE SILK DRAPERIES **COBWEBS.**

NOW - **HERE** ALL IS **REAL, SWEET,** AND **PURE.**

JANE, A **FLOWER.**

THIS **STRANGE NIGHT** HAS MADE YOU LOOK **PALE.** WERE YOU **AFRAID?**

I WAS **AFRAID** OF SOMEONE COMING OUT OF THE **INNER ROOM.**

BUT I HAD **FASTENED** THE **DOOR.**

I SHOULD HAVE BEEN A **CARELESS SHEPHERD** IF I HAD **LEFT** MY **PET LAMB** SO NEAR A **WOLF'S DEN, UNGUARDED.**

IS THE **DANGER** YOU **APPREHENDED** LAST NIGHT **GONE** BY NOW, SIR?

I CANNOT **VOUCH** FOR THAT TILL **MASON** IS OUT OF **ENGLAND: NOR** EVEN **THEN.**

HE DOESN'T **SEEM** ONE TO **WILFULLY INJURE** YOU.

OH NO! BUT, **UNINTENTIONALLY,** HE **MIGHT -** BY **ONE CARELESS WORD** - **DEPRIVE** ME FOR EVER OF **HAPPINESS.**

TELL HIM TO BE CAUTIOUS AND AVERT THE DANGER.

HA! I MUST KEEP HIM IGNORANT THAT HARM TO ME IS POSSIBLE!

NOW YOU LOOK PUZZLED; AND I WILL PUZZLE YOU FURTHER.

YOU ARE MY LITTLE FRIEND, ARE YOU NOT?

I LIKE TO SERVE AND OBEY YOU, SIR.

WELL THEN, SUPPOSE YOU WERE A WILD BOY, INDULGED FROM CHILDHOOD, IN A REMOTE FOREIGN LAND, AND YOU COMMIT A CAPITAL ERROR - MIND I DON'T SAY A CRIME - WHOSE CONSEQUENCES MUST FOLLOW YOU THROUGH LIFE AND TAINT ALL YOUR EXISTENCE.

YOU COME HOME AFTER YEARS OF VOLUNTARY BANISHMENT, AND MEET A STRANGER WITH THE GOOD QUALITIES YOU SOUGHT FOR TWENTY YEARS.

IS THE SINFUL, BUT REPENTANT, WANDERER JUSTIFIED IN DARING THE WORLD'S OPINION, IN ORDER TO ATTACH TO HIM FOR EVER THIS GENTLE, GRACIOUS, GENIAL STRANGER, THEREBY SECURING HIS OWN PEACE OF MIND?

SIR, A SINNER'S REFORMATION SHOULD NEVER DEPEND ON A FELLOW-CREATURE.

IF ANY YOU KNOW HAS SUFFERED AND ERRED, LET HIM LOOK HIGHER THAN HIS EQUALS FOR STRENGTH TO AMEND AND SOLACE TO HEAL.

GOD, WHO DOES THE WORK, ORDAINS THE INSTRUMENT!

I HAVE MYSELF BEEN A WORLDLY, DISSIPATED, RESTLESS MAN, AND I BELIEVE I HAVE FOUND THE INSTRUMENT FOR MY CURE IN --

-- MISS INGRAM!

DON'T YOU THINK IF I MARRIED HER SHE WOULD REGENERATE ME WITH A VENGEANCE?

JANE, YOU ARE QUITE PALE. DON'T YOU CURSE ME FOR DISTURBING YOUR REST?

CURSE YOU? NO, SIR.

~ CHAPTER XXI ~

THAT AFTERNOON I RECEIVED A VISITOR.

I DARESAY YOU HARDLY REMEMBER ME, MISS. MY NAME IS LEAVEN: I LIVED COACHMAN WITH MRS. REED WHEN YOU WERE AT GATESHEAD.

OH, ROBERT! I REMEMBER YOU VERY WELL.

HOW IS YOUR WIFE BESSIE, AND THE FAMILY AT THE HOUSE?

MY WIFE IS VERY HEARTY, THANK YOU. I AM SORRY TO SAY, MR. JOHN DIED LAST WEEK. HE RUINED HIS HEALTH AND HIS ESTATE WITH THE WORST MEN AND WOMEN. HE WAS IN DEBT, HIS MOTHER WOULDN'T HELP HIM, AND THEY SAY HE KILLED HIMSELF.

MISSIS HAD BEEN OUT OF HEALTH HERSELF FOR SOME TIME.

THE INFORMATION ABOUT MR. JOHN'S DEATH BROUGHT ON A STROKE.

SHE WAS THREE DAYS WITHOUT SPEAKING; BUT NOW SHE KEEPS SAYING TO BESSIE, "BRING JANE - FETCH JANE EYRE".

IF YOU CAN GET READY, MISS, I SHOULD LIKE TO TAKE YOU BACK WITH ME.

I WENT IN SEARCH OF MR. ROCHESTER, TO ASK FOR LEAVE OF ABSENCE.

DOES THAT PERSON WANT YOU?

I TOLD HIM ABOUT MRS. REED AND WHAT HAD HAPPENED.

...BUT GATESHEAD IS A HUNDRED MILES OFF! MRS. REED SENDS FOR PEOPLE TO SEE HER THAT DISTANCE? THERE WAS A REED OF GATESHEAD, A MAGISTRATE.

IT IS HIS WIDOW, SIR - AND MY UNCLE.

THE DEUCE HE WAS! YOU ALWAYS SAID YOU HAD NO RELATIONS.

NONE THAT WOULD OWN ME, SIR. SHE CAST ME OFF BECAUSE SHE DISLIKED ME; BUT THAT IS LONG AGO. I COULD NOT EASILY NEGLECT HER WISHES NOW.

I REACHED GATESHEAD ON THE FIRST OF MAY. THE SAME HOSTILE ROOF NOW ROSE BEFORE ME. I STILL FELT AS A WANDERER ON THE FACE OF THE EARTH; BUT I EXPERIENCED FIRMER TRUST IN MYSELF AND MY OWN POWERS. THE INANIMATE OBJECTS WERE NOT CHANGED; BUT THE LIVING THINGS HAD ALTERED PAST RECOGNITION.

HOW IS MRS. REED?

AH! MAMA, YOU MEAN; SHE IS EXTREMELY POORLY; I DOUBT IF YOU CAN SEE HER TONIGHT.

I MET BESSIE ON THE LANDING ON THE WAY TO MY CHAMBER, AND SHE TOOK ME TO SEE MRS. REED.

73

IS THIS JANE EYRE?

YES, AUNT REED.

I HAD **ONCE** VOWED THAT I WOULD **NEVER** CALL HER **AUNT AGAIN.**

I HAVE **TWICE** DONE YOU A **WRONG.**

READ THE LETTER.

ONE WAS BREAKING THE PROMISE TO MY **HUSBAND** TO BRING YOU **UP** AS MY **OWN** CHILD.

GO TO MY **DRESSING-CASE,** AND TAKE OUT A **LETTER** YOU WILL SEE THERE.

THE **OTHER** - WELL, **ETERNITY** IS BEFORE ME, I HAD **BETTER TELL HER.**

"MADAM, WILL YOU HAVE THE **GOODNESS** TO SEND ME THE **ADDRESS** OF MY NIECE, **JANE EYRE,** AND TELL ME HOW SHE **IS? PROVIDENCE** HAS **BLESSED** MY **ENDEAVOURS;** AND AS I AM **UNMARRIED** AND **CHILDLESS,** I WISH TO **ADOPT** HER, AND **BEQUEATH** HER AT MY **DEATH** WHATEVER I **HAVE** TO **LEAVE.**

- JOHN EYRE, MADEIRA."

THIS IS **THREE** YEARS OLD. WHY DID I NEVER **HEAR** OF THIS?

BECAUSE I **DISLIKED YOU** TOO **FIXEDLY** AND **THOROUGHLY EVER** TO LEND A **HAND** IN LIFTING YOU TO **PROSPERITY.**

I COULD NOT **FORGET** YOUR CONDUCT TO ME, **JANE** - THE **FURY** WITH WHICH YOU ONCE **TURNED** ON ME OR HOW THE **THOUGHT** OF ME MADE YOU **SICK.**

I TOOK MY REVENGE: I WROTE TO YOUR UNCLE AND **TOLD** HIM THAT JANE EYRE HAD DIED OF **TYPHUS FEVER** AT **LOWOOD.** NOW **ACT** AS YOU **PLEASE. EXPOSE** MY **FALSEHOOD.** YOU WERE **BORN,** I THINK, TO BE MY **TORMENT.**

*POOR, SUFFERING WOMAN! IT WAS **TOO LATE** FOR HER TO MAKE **NOW** THE **EFFORT** TO **CHANGE** HER HABITUAL **FRAME** OF MIND: LIVING, SHE HAD **EVER HATED** ME - DYING, SHE MUST **HATE** ME STILL.*

*A **STRANGE** AND **SOLEMN OBJECT** WAS THAT **CORPSE** TO ME. I GAZED ON IT WITH **GLOOM** AND **PAIN;** A GRATING **ANGUISH** FOR **HER WOES** - NOT **MY LOSS.***

WITH **HER** CONSTITUTION SHE SHOULD HAVE **LIVED** TO A **GOOD OLD AGE:** HER **LIFE** WAS **SHORTENED** BY **TROUBLE.**

A **MONTH** ELAPSED BEFORE I **QUITTED** GATESHEAD.

GEORGIANA MADE AN **ADVANTAGEOUS MATCH** WITH A **WEALTHY, WORN-OUT MAN** OF **FASHION**.

ELIZA TOOK THE **VEIL** AND IS AT THIS DAY **SUPERIOR** OF THE **CONVENT** WHERE SHE PASSED THE **PERIOD** OF HER **NOVITIATE**, AND WHICH SHE **ENDOWED** WITH HER **FORTUNE**.

~ CHAPTER XXII ~

MY **RETURN JOURNEY** TO **THORNFIELD** SEEMED **TEDIOUS**. I FELT **GLAD** AS THE ROAD **SHORTENED** BEFORE ME. IT WAS **PLEASURE** ENOUGH TO HAVE THE **PRIVILEGE** OF AGAIN **LOOKING** AT **MR. ROCHESTER**, WHETHER HE **LOOKED** ON ME OR **NOT**.

HASTEN! BE **WITH** HIM WHILE YOU **MAY**: BUT A FEW **MORE DAYS** OR **WEEKS**, AT **MOST**, AND YOU ARE **PARTED** FROM HIM FOR **EVER!**

HOLLO!

THERE YOU ARE!

AND **THIS** IS **JANE EYRE**? COMING FROM **MILLCOTE**, AND ON **FOOT**?

YES - JUST ONE OF YOUR **TRICKS**: TO **STEAL** INTO THE **VICINAGE** OF YOUR **HOME** ALONG WITH **TWILIGHT**, JUST AS IF YOU WERE A **DREAM**.

WHAT THE **DEUCE** HAVE YOU **DONE** WITH YOURSELF THIS LAST **MONTH**?

I HAVE **BEEN** WITH MY **AUNT**, SIR, WHO IS **DEAD**.

A **TRUE JANIAN REPLY!** SHE **COMES** FROM THE **OTHER WORLD** - FROM THE **ABODE** OF **PEOPLE** WHO ARE **DEAD**; AND **TELLS ME SO** WHEN SHE MEETS ME **ALONE** HERE IN THE **GLOAMING!**

IF I **DARED**, I'D **TOUCH** YOU, TO SEE IF YOU ARE **SUBSTANCE** OR **SHADOW**, YOU **ELF!**

TRUANT! ABSENT FROM ME A **WHOLE MONTH**, AND **FORGETTING** ME **QUITE**, I'LL BE **SWORN**.

I KNEW THERE WOULD BE PLEASURE IN MEETING MY MASTER AGAIN.

HAVE YOU NOT BEEN TO **LONDON** TO BUY A NEW **CARRIAGE?**

YES; I SUPPOSE YOU FOUND **THAT** OUT BY **SECOND-SIGHT**. YOU MUST **SEE** THE **CARRIAGE**, **JANE**, AND **TELL** ME IF YOU DON'T THINK IT WILL **SUIT** MRS. **ROCHESTER** EXACTLY.

I WISH I WERE A TRIFLE BETTER **ADAPTED** TO **MATCH** WITH HER **EXTERNALLY**.

FAIRY AS YOU **ARE**, CAN'T YOU GIVE ME A **CHARM** TO MAKE ME A **HANDSOME MAN?**

IT WOULD BE **PAST** THE **POWER** OF **MAGIC**, SIR.

A **LOVING EYE** IS ALL THE **CHARM** NEEDED.

STAY YOUR **WEARY** LITTLE WANDERING FEET AT A **FRIEND'S THRESHOLD**.

THANK YOU, MR. **ROCHESTER,** FOR YOUR **GREAT KINDNESS**. I AM STRANGELY **GLAD** TO GET **BACK AGAIN** TO YOU.

WHEREVER YOU **ARE** IS MY **HOME** - MY ONLY **HOME**.

ADÈLE WAS HALF **WILD** WITH **DELIGHT** WHEN SHE **SAW** ME. MRS. **FAIRFAX** RECEIVED ME WITH HER **USUAL FRIENDLINESS**.

THERE IS NO **HAPPINESS** LIKE THAT OF BEING **LOVED** BY YOUR **FELLOW-CREATURES;** AND, **ALAS!** NEVER HAD I LOVED **HIM** SO **WELL**.

~ CHAPTER XXIII ~

ON **MIDSUMMER-EVE,** **ADÈLE, WEARY** WITH GATHERING **WILD STRAWBERRIES,** HAD GONE TO **BED** WITH THE **SUN**. I WATCHED HER DROP ASLEEP, AND WHEN I **LEFT** HER, I SOUGHT THE **GARDEN**.

THIS **SCENT** IS NEITHER **SHRUB** NOR **FLOWER**.

I KNOW IT **WELL** - IT IS MR. **ROCHESTER'S CIGAR**.

I MADE NO *NOISE*: HE HAD NOT *EYES* BEHIND — COULD HIS *SHADOW* FEEL?

JANE, COME AND LOOK AT *THIS FELLOW.* LOOK AT HIS *WINGS.* HE *REMINDS* ME RATHER OF A *WEST INDIAN* INSECT.

JANE, *THORNFIELD* IS A *PLEASANT PLACE* IN *SUMMER,* IS IT *NOT?*

YES, SIR.

YOU *MUST* HAVE BECOME IN *SOME* DEGREE *ATTACHED* TO THE HOUSE.

I AM *ATTACHED* TO IT, INDEED.

PITY. IT IS ALWAYS THE *WAY* OF *EVENTS* IN THIS *LIFE.*

NO *SOONER* HAVE YOU GOT *SETTLED,* THAN A *VOICE* CALLS *OUT* TO YOU TO *MOVE ON.*

MUST I *MOVE ON,* SIR? MUST I *LEAVE THORNFIELD?*

I BELIEVE YOU *MUST,* JANE.

IN A *MONTH* I *HOPE* TO BE A *BRIDEGROOM.* *ADÈLE* MUST GO TO *SCHOOL;* AND YOU, *MISS EYRE,* MUST GET A *NEW SITUATION.* I HAVE *ALREADY,* THROUGH MY *FUTURE MOTHER-IN-LAW,* HEARD OF A *PLACE* THAT I THINK WILL *SUIT:*

TO UNDERTAKE THE *EDUCATION* OF *FIVE DAUGHTERS* OF A *MRS. O'GALL* OF *CONNAUGHT,* IRELAND. YOU'LL *LIKE* IRELAND, I THINK: THEY'RE SUCH *WARM-HEARTED PEOPLE* THERE, THEY *SAY.*

IT IS A *LONG WAY OFF,* SIR.

A GIRL OF *YOUR SENSE* WILL NOT OBJECT TO THE *VOYAGE* OR THE *DISTANCE.*

NOT THE *VOYAGE,* BUT THE *DISTANCE:* AND THEN THE *SEA* IS A *BARRIER* --

FROM *WHAT,* JANE?

-- FROM *ENGLAND* AND FROM *THORNFIELD;* AND --

-- FROM *YOU,* SIR.

WE HAVE BEEN *GOOD FRIENDS,* JANE; AND WHEN *FRIENDS* ARE ON THE *EVE* OF *SEPARATION,* THEY *LIKE* TO SPEND THE *LITTLE TIME* THAT *REMAINS* TO THEM *CLOSE* TO EACH OTHER.

I *SOMETIMES* HAVE A *QUEER FEELING* WITH *REGARD* TO YOU — *ESPECIALLY* WHEN YOU ARE *NEAR ME,* AS *NOW:*

IT IS AS *IF* I HAVE A *STRING* SOMEWHERE UNDER MY *LEFT RIBS,* TIGHTLY AND *INEXTRICABLY KNOTTED* TO A *SIMILAR* STRING SITUATED IN THE *CORRESPONDING QUARTER* OF *YOUR* LITTLE FRAME.

AND IF THAT **BOISTEROUS CHANNEL,** AND TWO HUNDRED **MILES** OR SO OF **LAND** COME **BROAD** BETWEEN US, I AM **AFRAID** THAT **CORD** OF **COMMUNION** WILL BE **SNAPPED;** AND **THEN** I'VE A **NERVOUS NOTION** I SHOULD **TAKE** TO **BLEEDING INWARDLY.**

AS FOR **YOU,** - YOU'D **FORGET** ME.

THAT I **NEVER** SHOULD, SIR.

JANE, DO YOU HEAR THAT **NIGHTINGALE** SINGING?

I **WISH** -sob- I HAD -sob- **NEVER COME** TO **THORNFIELD.**

I -sob- **WISH** -sob- I HAD **NEVER EVER** -sob- **BEEN BORN.**

BECAUSE YOU ARE **SORRY** TO **LEAVE** IT?

I **GRIEVE** TO LEAVE THORNFIELD: I **LOVE** THORNFIELD, BECAUSE I HAVE **LIVED** IN IT A **FULL LIFE** AND HAVE NOT BEEN **TRAMPLED** ON.

I HAVE **TALKED** WITH AN **ORIGINAL, EXPANDED MIND** - YOU, MR. **ROCHESTER.**

I SEE THE **NECESSITY** OF **DEPARTURE;** AND IT IS LIKE **LOOKING** ON THE **NECESSITY** OF **DEATH.**

WHERE DO YOU SEE THE **NECESSITY?**

DO YOU **THINK** I CAN **STAY** TO BECOME **NOTHING** TO YOU? DO YOU **THINK** I AM A **MACHINE** WITHOUT **FEELINGS?** DO YOU THINK BECAUSE I AM **POOR** AND **PLAIN,** I AM **SOULLESS** AND **HEARTLESS?** I HAVE AS MUCH **SOUL** AS YOU - AND **FULL** AS MUCH **HEART!**

IT IS MY **SPIRIT** THAT ADDRESSES **YOUR** SPIRIT NOW --

-- JUST AS IF **BOTH** HAD **PASSED** THROUGH THE **GRAVE** AND **STOOD** AT **GOD'S FEET,** EQUAL - AS WE **ARE!**

AS WE **ARE!** SO - SO, JANE!

YET NOT SO, FOR **YOU** ARE **AS GOOD** AS **MARRIED** TO AN **INFERIOR** WHOM YOU **DO NOT** LOVE.

I **SCORN** SUCH A **UNION:** THEREFORE I AM **BETTER** THAN YOU --

-- LET ME GO!

JANE, DON'T **STRUGGLE** SO.

78

YOUR WILL SHALL **DECIDE** YOUR **DESTINY.** I OFFER YOU MY **HAND,** MY **HEART,** AND A **SHARE** OF ALL MY **POSSESSIONS.**

JANE, I **SUMMON** YOU AS MY **WIFE.** IT IS **YOU ONLY** I INTEND TO **MARRY.**

YOU PLAY A **FARCE,** WHICH I MERELY **LAUGH AT.** YOUR **BRIDE** STANDS BETWEEN US.

MY **BRIDE** IS **HERE,** BECAUSE MY **EQUAL** IS **HERE,** AND MY **LIKENESS.**

WHAT **LOVE** HAVE **I** FOR MISS INGRAM? **NONE:** AND **THAT** YOU KNOW.

WHAT **LOVE** HAS **SHE** FOR **ME?** **NONE.**

I **CAUSED** A **RUMOUR** TO REACH HER THAT MY **FORTUNE** WAS **FAR LESS** THAN SHE **THOUGHT;** AND SHE TURNED **COLD** TOWARDS ME. I **WOULD NOT** MARRY MISS INGRAM.

YOU **STRANGE,** ALMOST **UNEARTHLY** THING, I **LOVE YOU** AS MY **OWN** FLESH. I MUST **HAVE YOU** FOR MY **OWN** - **ENTIRELY** MY **OWN.**

JANE, WILL YOU **MARRY ME?**

MR. **ROCHESTER,** LET ME **LOOK** AT YOUR **FACE.**

TURN TO THE **MOONLIGHT,** BECAUSE I WANT TO **READ** YOUR COUNTENANCE.

MAKE **HASTE,** FOR I **SUFFER.**

DO YOU **SINCERELY** WISH ME TO BE YOUR **WIFE?**

I **DO,** I **SWEAR** IT.

THEN, **SIR,** I **WILL** MARRY YOU.

EDWARD --

-- MY **LITTLE WIFE!**

DEAR **EDWARD!**

KRAKK OOOMM!!

GOD PARDON ME! AND **MAN MEDDLE NOT** WITH ME: I **HAVE HER,** AND WILL **HOLD HER.**

AGAIN AND **AGAIN,** HE SAID, "ARE YOU **HAPPY, JANE?"** AND **AGAIN** AND **AGAIN** I ANSWERED, "YES."

A BRILLIANT JUNE MORNING HAD SUCCEEDED TO THE TEMPEST OF THE NIGHT. I HASTENED TO MEET WITH MR. ROCHESTER.

WHY DID YOU TAKE SUCH **PAINS** TO MAKE ME **BELIEVE** YOU WISHED TO **MARRY** MISS INGRAM?

ALTHOUGH I SHOULD MAKE YOU A LITTLE **INDIGNANT** - AND I HAVE **SEEN** WHAT A **FIRE-SPIRIT** YOU CAN BE - YOU **GLOWED** IN THE **COOL MOONLIGHT** LAST NIGHT, WHEN YOU **MUTINIED** AGAINST FATE, AND CLAIMED YOUR RANK AS MY **EQUAL**.

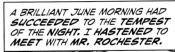

~ CHAPTER XXIV ~

I FEIGNED COURTSHIP OF **MISS INGRAM** BECAUSE I **WISHED** TO **RENDER** YOU AS **MADLY** IN **LOVE** WITH ME AS I **WAS** WITH **YOU;** AND I KNEW **JEALOUSY** WOULD BE THE **BEST ALLY** I COULD CALL IN FOR THE **FURTHERANCE** OF THAT **END**.

DID YOU THINK **NOTHING** OF **MISS INGRAM'S** FEELINGS, SIR?

HER **FEELINGS** ARE CONCENTRATED IN **ONE - PRIDE;** AND **THAT** NEEDS **HUMBLING**.

YOU HAVE A **CURIOUS, DESIGNING** MIND, MR. ROCHESTER. I AM **AFRAID** YOUR **PRINCIPLES** ON **SOME** POINTS ARE **ECCENTRIC**.

MY **PRINCIPLES** WERE **NEVER TRAINED,** JANE; THEY **MAY** HAVE GROWN A LITTLE **AWRY** FOR **WANT** OF **ATTENTION**.

I **LOVED** HIM **VERY MUCH** - MORE THAN **WORDS** HAD **POWER** TO **EXPRESS**.

WE AGREED ON A **QUIET** WEDDING, BUT I FELT I SHOULD **WRITE** TO MY **UNCLE JOHN** IN **MADEIRA** TO **TELL** HIM ABOUT MY **MARRIAGE**.

~ CHAPTER XXV ~

THE **HURRY** OF **PREPARATION** FOR THE **BRIDAL DAY,** AND THE **ANTICIPATION** OF THE **GREAT CHANGE** MADE ME **FEVERISH.** ONE **NIGHT,** WHEN MR. ROCHESTER WAS **ABSENT** FROM **HOME,** MY **ANXIOUS EXCITEMENT** CONTINUED IN **DREAMS**.

THAT **SAME NIGHT,** I **WOKE** TO SEE A **GHOST** WEARING MY **WEDDING-DRESS** AND **VEIL.**

MY **BLOOD** CREPT **COLD** THROUGH MY **VEINS.** THE **SHAPE BEFORE ME** HAD **NEVER** CROSSED MY **EYES** BEFORE; THE **HEIGHT,** THE **CONTOUR** WERE **NEW** TO ME. IT WAS **NOT** EVEN THAT **STRANGE** WOMAN, **GRACE POOLE.**

I LOST **CONSCIOUSNESS** AND BECAME **INSENSIBLE** WITH **TERROR.**

THE **TRANSACTION ACTUALLY TOOK PLACE.** ON **RISING,** I SAW THE **VEIL** ON THE **CARPET.** IT WAS **TORN** FROM **TOP** TO **BOTTOM** AND IN **TWO HALVES!**

I **WAITED** NOW **MR. ROCHESTER'S RETURN.** I WAS **EAGER** TO **DISBURTHEN** MY **MIND,** AND TO **SEEK** OF HIM THE **SOLUTION** OF THE **ENIGMA** THAT **PERPLEXED** ME.

A WOMAN **DID,** I **DOUBT** NOT, ENTER YOUR ROOM: AND **THAT** WOMAN **MUST** HAVE BEEN **GRACE POOLE.** I **SEE** YOU WOULD **ASK** WHY I **KEEP** SUCH A WOMAN IN MY **HOUSE:**

WHEN WE HAVE BEEN **MARRIED** A YEAR AND A **DAY,** I WILL **TELL YOU,** BUT NOT **NOW.**

ARE YOU **SATISFIED,** JANE? DO YOU **ACCEPT** MY **SOLUTION** OF THE **MYSTERY?**

SATISFIED I WAS **NOT,** BUT TO **PLEASE** HIM I **ENDEAVOURED** TO BE SO - **RELIEVED,** I CERTAINLY **DID FEEL.**

MR. ROCHESTER **INSISTED** I **SLEEP** THAT NIGHT IN THE **NURSERY** WITH THE **DOOR BOLTED.** SOPHIE WAS TO **ROUSE ME** IN **GOOD TIME** FOR OUR **WEDDING** IN THE MORNING. WITH LITTLE **ADÈLE** IN MY ARMS, I WATCHED THE **SLUMBER** OF **CHILDHOOD** AND **WAITED** FOR THE **COMING DAY;** SHE SEEMED THE **EMBLEM** OF MY **PAST LIFE.**

~ CHAPTER XXVI ~

...WILT THOU **HAVE** THIS **WOMAN** FOR THY **WEDDED WIFE**?

THE MARRIAGE CANNOT **GO ON:** I DECLARE THE **EXISTENCE** OF AN **IMPEDIMENT.**

PROCEED.

I CANNOT **PROCEED** WITHOUT SOME **INVESTIGATION** - PERHAPS THIS IMPEDIMENT MAY BE **EXPLAINED AWAY?**

HARDLY! MR. ROCHESTER HAS A **WIFE** NOW **LIVING.**

FAVOUR ME WITH AN **ACCOUNT** OF HER.

MY NAME IS **BRIGGS** - A **SOLICITOR** OF **LONDON** - AND I HAVE A **WITNESS.**

MR. **MASON,** HAVE THE **GOODNESS** TO STEP **FORWARD.**

WHAT HAVE **YOU** TO SAY?

GOOD **GOD!**

THE **DEVIL** IS **IN** IT IF YOU CANNOT **ANSWER DISTINCTLY.**

SIR, DO NOT **FORGET** YOU ARE IN A **SACRED PLACE.**

COURAGE. SPEAK **OUT.**

SHE IS **NOW LIVING** AT **THORNFIELD HALL.** I SAW HER THERE LAST **APRIL.** I'M HER **BROTHER.**

NO, BY GOD!

ENOUGH! THERE WILL BE **NO WEDDING TO-DAY.** BIGAMY IS AN **UGLY WORD!** - I **MEANT,** HOWEVER, TO **BE A BIGAMIST;**

BUT **FATE** HAS **OUT-MANOEUVRED** ME, OR **PROVIDENCE CHECKED** ME. I'M **LITTLE** BETTER THAN A **DEVIL** AT THIS **MOMENT;** AND **DESERVE,** NO **DOUBT,** THE **STERNEST** JUDGMENTS OF GOD.

A **LUNATIC** IS KEPT UNDER **WATCH** AT **THORNFIELD.** SHE IS MY **WIFE,** WHOM I **MARRIED FIFTEEN YEARS** AGO.

BERTHA **MASON** BY NAME; **SISTER** OF THIS **RESOLUTE PERSONAGE.**

CHEER UP, **DICK!** I'D **ALMOST** AS **SOON** STRIKE A **WOMAN** AS **YOU.**

BERTHA MASON IS **MAD;** AND SHE **CAME** OF A **MAD FAMILY; IDIOTS** AND **MANIACS** THROUGH **THREE GENERATIONS!** - AS I FOUND OUT **AFTER** I HAD WED THE **DAUGHTER.**

BERTHA, LIKE A **DUTIFUL CHILD,** COPIED HER **MOTHER** BY BEING A **MADWOMAN** AND A **DRUNKARD.**

OH, I WENT THROUGH **RICH SCENES!**

THIS **GIRL** KNEW **NO MORE** THAN **YOU** OF THE **DISGUSTING SECRET**: SHE **THOUGHT** ALL WAS **FAIR** AND **LEGAL**, AND NEVER **DREAMT** SHE WAS GOING TO BE **ENTRAPPED** INTO A **FEIGNED UNION** WITH A DEFRAUDED **WRETCH**, ALREADY **BOUND** TO A **BAD**, **MAD**, AND **EMBRUTED** PARTNER!

BRIGGS, **WOOD**, **MASON**, I INVITE YOU **ALL** TO COME UP TO THE **HOUSE** AND VISIT **MRS. POOLE'S** PATIENT, AND **MY WIFE!**

YOU SHALL **SEE** WHAT SORT OF **BEING** I WAS **CHEATED** INTO **ESPOUSING**, AND **JUDGE** WHETHER OR **NOT** I HAD A **RIGHT** TO **BREAK** THE **COMPACT**, AND SEEK **SYMPATHY** WITH **SOMETHING** AT **LEAST** *HUMAN.*

YOU KNOW THIS PLACE, **MASON** - SHE BIT AND **STABBED** YOU HERE.

GOOD MORNING, MRS. **POOLE!** HOW ARE **YOU** AND YOUR **CHARGE** TO-DAY?

WE'RE **TOLERABLE**, SIR, **THANK** YOU.

RATHER **SNAPPISH**, BUT NOT **'RAGEOUS.**

EE-AHH-AHHH!

SHE HAS NO **KNIFE** NOW, I SUPPOSE?

ONE **NEVER** KNOWS **WHAT** SHE HAS, SIR.

FOR **GOD'S SAKE,** TAKE CARE!

We had better leave her.

GO TO THE **DEVIL!**

YEE-AH! YAH-OH EE-UHH!

THIS IS MY **WIFE.**

GRRR! GRARRGH!

SUCH IS THE **SOLE CONJUGAL** EMBRACE I AM EVER TO KNOW --

-- SUCH ARE THE **ENDEARMENTS** WHICH ARE TO **SOLACE** MY LEISURE HOURS!

AND **THIS** IS WHAT I **WISHED** TO HAVE,

THIS **YOUNG GIRL,** WHO STANDS SO **GRAVE** AND **QUIET** AT THE **MOUTH** OF **HELL.**

LOOK AT THE **DIFFERENCE!**

THEN **JUDGE ME, PRIEST** OF THE **GOSPEL** AND **MAN** OF THE **LAW,** AND **REMEMBER** WITH WHAT **JUDGMENT** YE **JUDGE,** YE SHALL BE **JUDGED!**

YOU, MADAM, ARE CLEARED FROM **ALL BLAME**: YOUR **UNCLE** WILL BE **GLAD** TO **HEAR** IT - IF, INDEED, HE IS **STILL LIVING.**

MY **UNCLE!** DO YOU **KNOW** HIM?

MR. MASON WAS **WITH** HIM AT **MADEIRA** WHEN HE RECEIVED YOUR **LETTER** INTIMATING THE CONTEMPLATED UNION.

MR. MASON **REVEALED** THE **REAL STATE** OF MATTERS.

YOUR **UNCLE** IS NOW ON A **SICK-BED,** BUT **IMPLORED** MR. MASON TO **PREVENT** THE **FALSE MARRIAGE.**

THE HOUSE CLEARED. I SHUT MYSELF IN AND PROCEEDED - NOT TO WEEP, NOT TO MOURN, BUT - MECHANICALLY TO TAKE OFF THE WEDDING-DRESS, AND REPLACE IT BY THE GOWN I WORE YESTERDAY; YET WHERE WAS THE JANE EYRE OF YESTERDAY? WHERE WAS HER LIFE? WHERE WERE HER PROSPECTS? I SANK IN DEEP MIRE; THE FLOODS OVERFLOWED ME.

~ CHAPTER ~
~ XXVII ~

WELL, **JANE!** NO WORD OF **REPROACH?** NOTHING **BITTER?** I NEVER **MEANT** TO **WOUND** YOU THUS!

WILL YOU **EVER FORGIVE ME?**

I **FORGAVE HIM** AT THE **MOMENT** AND ON THE **SPOT.** THERE WAS SUCH **DEEP REMORSE** IN HIS EYE, SUCH **UNCHANGED LOVE** IN HIS **WHOLE LOOK. I FORGAVE** HIM **ALL:** YET **NOT** IN **WORDS,** NOT **OUTWARDLY;** ONLY AT MY **HEART'S CORE.**

YOU **KNOW** I AM A **SCOUNDREL,** JANE?

YES, SIR.

THEN **TELL ME** SO **ROUNDLY. SHARPLY.**

I **CANNOT:** I AM **TIRED** AND **SICK.**

IF I COULD **GO OUT** OF LIFE **NOW,** IT WOULD BE **WELL** FOR ME. THEN I SHOULD NOT HAVE TO **CRACK MY HEART-STRINGS** IN RENDING THEM FROM **MR. ROCHESTER'S.**

I **MUST** LEAVE HIM.
I **DO NOT WANT** TO LEAVE HIM.
I **CANNOT** LEAVE HIM.

YOU **INTEND** TO **MAKE** YOURSELF A COMPLETE **STRANGER** TO ME.

ALL IS **CHANGED** ABOUT ME, SIR: I MUST CHANGE **TOO.**

ADÈLE MUST HAVE A **NEW GOVERNESS,** SIR.

ADÈLE WILL GO TO **SCHOOL** - I HAVE **SETTLED** THAT **ALREADY.**

I WAS **WRONG** TO **BRING** YOU HERE. I **FEARED** A GOVERNESS WOULD NEVER **STAY** IF SHE HAD KNOWLEDGE OF THE **CURSE;** AND MY **PLANS** WOULD NOT **PERMIT** ME TO **REMOVE** THE **MANIAC** ELSEWHERE --

...THOUGH I **POSSESS** AN **OLD HOUSE, FERNDEAN MANOR,** WHERE I **COULD** HAVE LODGED HER. **PROBABLY** THOSE **DAMP WALLS** WOULD HAVE SOON **EASED** ME OF HER **CHARGE.** MY **CONSCIENCE RECOILED** FROM THE **ARRANGEMENT.**

I'LL **SHUT UP THORNFIELD HALL:** I'LL GIVE MRS. POOLE TWO HUNDRED A YEAR TO BE AT HAND WHEN MY **WIFE** IS **PROMPTED** BY HER **FAMILIAR** TO **BURN** PEOPLE IN THEIR **BEDS, STAB** AND **BITE** THEIR **FLESH,** AND **SO ON...**

SIR, YOU **SPEAK** OF HER WITH **HATE**.

IT IS **CRUEL** - SHE CANNOT **HELP** BEING **MAD**.

JANE, MY LITTLE **DARLING**, YOU **MISJUDGE** ME AGAIN:

IT IS **NOT** BECAUSE SHE IS **MAD** I HATE HER. IF **YOU** WERE **MAD**, DO YOU THINK I SHOULD **HATE** YOU?

I **DO** INDEED, SIR.

THEN YOU ARE **MISTAKEN**, AND YOU KNOW **NOTHING** ABOUT **ME** AND **NOTHING** ABOUT THE SORT OF **LOVE** OF WHICH I AM **CAPABLE**.

EVERY **ATOM** OF YOUR **FLESH** IS AS **DEAR** TO ME AS MY **OWN**. I SHOULD NOT **SHRINK** FROM YOU WITH **DISGUST** AS I DID FROM **HER**.

I COULD **NEVER WEARY** OF GAZING INTO YOUR EYES, THOUGH THEY HAD **NO LONGER A RAY** OF **RECOGNITION** FOR ME.

JANE! JANE! YOU **DON'T LOVE** ME, THEN?

I **DO** LOVE YOU - MORE THAN **EVER**: BUT I **MUST NOT** SHOW OR INDULGE THE FEELING;

AND **THIS** IS THE **LAST TIME** I MUST **EXPRESS** IT --

-- AND **THEREFORE**, MR. ROCHESTER, I MUST **LEAVE** YOU.

FOR **HOW LONG**, JANE?

I MUST **PART** WITH YOU FOR MY **WHOLE LIFE**: I MUST BEGIN A **NEW EXISTENCE**.

OF **COURSE**. I PASS OVER THE **MADNESS** ABOUT **PARTING** FROM ME.

I AM **NOT MARRIED**.

YOU SHALL BE **MRS. ROCHESTER** AND **LIVE** IN A **VILLA** I HAVE IN THE SOUTH OF **FRANCE**.

SIR, YOUR **WIFE** IS **LIVING**: THAT IS A **FACT** ACKNOWLEDGED THIS **MORNING** BY YOURSELF.

IF I **LIVED** WITH YOU AS YOU **DESIRE** - I SHOULD THEN BE YOUR **MISTRESS**: TO SAY **OTHERWISE** IS SOPHISTICAL - IS **FALSE**.

JANE, I AM NOT A GENTLE-TEMPERED MAN - BEWARE!

WILL YOU HEAR **REASON**? BECAUSE, IF YOU **WON'T**, I'LL TRY **VIOLENCE**.

I **SAW** THAT **ONE PASSING SECOND** OF TIME WAS **ALL** I HAD TO **RESTRAIN** HIM. I WAS NOT **AFRAID**; I FELT AN **INWARD POWER**, A SENSE OF **INFLUENCE**, WHICH **SUPPORTED** ME.

SIT DOWN; I'LL **TALK** TO YOU AS **LONG** AS YOU **LIKE**, AND **HEAR** ALL YOU HAVE TO **SAY**.

I AM NOT **ANGRY**, JANE: I ONLY **LOVE YOU** TOO **WELL**;

AND YOU HAD **STEELED** YOUR **LITTLE PALE FACE** WITH SUCH A **RESOLUTE**, **FROZEN LOOK**, I COULD NOT **ENDURE** IT.

HUSH NOW.

JUST **PUT** YOUR **HAND** IN **MINE**, AND I WILL **SHOW** YOU THE **REAL STATE** OF THE **CASE**. CAN YOU **LISTEN** TO ME?

YES SIR; FOR **HOURS**, IF YOU **WILL**.

MY **FATHER** WAS AN **AVARICIOUS**, **GRASPING** MAN WHO COULD NOT **BEAR** THE **IDEA** OF DIVIDING HIS ESTATE: **ALL**, HE RESOLVED, SHOULD GO TO MY **BROTHER**, ROWLAND.

YET AS **LITTLE** COULD HE **ENDURE** THAT A **SON** OF **HIS** SHOULD BE A **POOR MAN**.

NOW THAT YOU HAVE **LEFT COLLEGE**, EDWARD, YOU MUST GO TO A **BUSINESS PARTNER** I'VE **FOUND** FOR YOU - A **PLANTER** AND MERCHANT IN **JAMAICA**.

HIS **DAUGHTER** BERTHA IS THE **BOAST** OF SPANISH TOWN FOR HER **BEAUTY**.

THIS WAS **NO LIE**; THOUGH MY **FATHER** SAID **NOTHING** ABOUT BERTHA MASON'S FORTUNE OF **THIRTY THOUSAND POUNDS**. MY **BRIDE** HAD **ALREADY** BEEN **COURTED** FOR ME.

HER *FAMILY* WISHED TO *SECURE ME*, BECAUSE I WAS OF A *GOOD RACE*; AND SO DID SHE. THEY *SHOWED HER* TO ME IN *PARTIES*, SPLENDIDLY DRESSED. I WAS DAZZLED: I *THOUGHT* I *LOVED* HER.

THE HONEYMOON *OVER*, I *LEARNED* MY *MISTAKE*; MY *BRIDE'S MOTHER* WAS *SHUT UP* IN A *LUNATIC ASYLUM*, AND THERE WAS A *YOUNGER, DUMB IDIOT*, OF A *BROTHER*.

COMPETITORS PIQUED ME: SHE *ALLURED* ME: A *MARRIAGE* WAS ACHIEVED ALMOST *BEFORE* I *KNEW* WHERE I *WAS*. I DID NOT EVEN *KNOW* HER.

MY *FATHER* AND *BROTHER* KNEW ALL THIS; BUT THEY *ONLY* THOUGHT OF THE *MONEY*, AND *JOINED* IN THE *PLOT* AGAINST ME.

I LIVED WITH THAT WOMAN *FOUR YEARS*, AND *BEFORE* THAT TIME SHE HAD *TRIED* ME *INDEED*. I COULD NOT PASS A *SINGLE HOUR* WITH HER IN *COMFORT*. NO *SERVANT* WOULD *BEAR* THE OUTBREAKS OF HER *VIOLENCE* AND *UNREASONABLE* TEMPER. I COULD NOT *LEGALLY* RID MYSELF OF HER FOR THE *DOCTORS* DECLARED HER AS *MAD*.

BOOOMMM!!!

F@!? EDWARD ROCHESTER! *?€*? *?!?!!! ...!€* EDWARD! §*?!

THIS *LIFE* IS *HELL* - I HAVE A *RIGHT* TO *DELIVER MYSELF* FROM IT.

LET ME *BREAK AWAY*, AND *GO HOME* TO *GOD!*

I ONLY *ENTERTAINED* THE *INTENTION* FOR A MOMENT.

AS I *WALKED* IN MY *WET GARDEN*, I SAW *HOPE REVIVE* - AND FELT *REGENERATION* POSSIBLE. *"RETURN TO EUROPE!"* SAID HOPE. *"YOUR FILTHY BURDEN* IS *NOT KNOWN* THERE. *SHELTER* HER *DEGRADATION* WITH *SECRECY*; AND *LEAVE HER."* MY *FATHER*, ANXIOUS TO *CONCEAL* THE CONNECTION, *HELPED* ME TO HIDE HER AT THORNFIELD HALL.

MY *BROTHER* IN THE *INTERVAL* WAS *DEAD*, AND MY *FATHER* SOON DIED *TOO*.

FOR *TEN LONG YEARS* I ROVE ABOUT. WITH *PLENTY* OF MONEY, I COULD CHOOSE MY OWN *SOCIETY*. NO *CIRCLES* WERE *CLOSED AGAINST* ME. AROUND THE *CITIES* OF EUROPE, I SOUGHT *HER* WHO *SUITED* ME.

WELL, SIR? DID YOU **FIND** ANYONE YOU **LIKED?**

I DID **NOT** - YET I **COULD NOT** LIVE ALONE;

SO I **TRIED** THE COMPANIONSHIP OF **MISTRESSES.**

THE **FIRST** I CHOSE WAS CÉLINE VARENS - YOU **ALREADY** KNOW HOW **THAT** LIAISON TERMINATED.

SHE HAD **TWO** SUCCESSORS.

HIRING A **MISTRESS** IS THE **NEXT WORSE THING** TO BUYING A **SLAVE:**

BOTH ARE OFTEN BY **NATURE,** AND **ALWAYS BY POSITION,** INFERIOR: AND TO LIVE **FAMILIARLY** WITH **INFERIORS** IS **DEGRADING.**

I **DREW** FROM THESE **WORDS** THAT WERE **I** TO BE THEIR **SUCCESSOR,** HE WOULD **ONE** DAY **REGARD ME** WITH THE **SAME FEELING.**

LAST **JANUARY,** RID OF ALL MY **MISTRESSES,** I **RETURNED** TO ENGLAND, **SOURLY DISPOSED** AGAINST **ALL WOMANKIND.**

RIDING ON A **FROSTY WINTER AFTERNOON,** I SAW A **QUIET LITTLE FIGURE** SITTING BY **ITSELF;** AND ON THE **OCCASION** OF MY **HORSE'S ACCIDENT,** IT **CAME UP** AND GRAVELY OFFERED ME **HELP.**

IT **SEEMED** AS IF A **LINNET** HAD **HOPPED** TO MY **FOOT** AND PROPOSED TO **BEAR ME** ON ITS TINY **WING.**

I WAS **SURLY;** BUT THE THING **WOULD NOT GO:** IT STOOD **BY** ME WITH **STRANGE PERSEVERANCE,** AND SPOKE WITH A SORT OF **AUTHORITY:** I MUST BE **AIDED,** AND BY **THAT HAND:** AND **AIDED** I WAS. WHEN **ONCE** I HAD PRESSED THE **FRAIL SHOULDER,** SOMETHING **NEW** STOLE INTO MY **FRAME.**

YOU **SEE NOW** HOW THE **CASE STANDS** - DO YOU **NOT?** I **HAVE** FOR THE FIRST TIME **FOUND** WHAT I CAN **TRULY LOVE** - I HAVE **FOUND YOU.**

YOU **UNDERSTAND** WHAT I **WANT** OF YOU? JUST THIS **PROMISE** - "**I WILL BE YOURS, MR. ROCHESTER.**"

MR. **ROCHESTER,** I WILL **NOT** BE YOURS.

JANE, DO YOU MEAN TO GO ONE WAY IN THE WORLD, AND TO LET ME GO ANOTHER?

I DO.

OH, JANE, THIS IS BITTER! THIS - THIS IS WICKED. IT WOULD NOT BE WICKED TO LOVE ME.

IT WOULD TO OBEY YOU.

WHAT SHALL I DO, JANE? WHERE TURN FOR A COMPANION, AND FOR SOME HOPE?

DO AS I DO: TRUST IN GOD, AND YOURSELF. BELIEVE IN HEAVEN. HOPE TO MEET AGAIN THERE.

YOU CONDEMN ME TO LIVE WRETCHED, AND TO DIE ACCURSED.

I ADVISE YOU TO LIVE SINLESS, AND I WISH YOU TO DIE TRANQUIL.

NEVER WAS ANYTHING AT ONCE SO FRAIL AND SO INDOMITABLE.

WHATEVER I DO WITH ITS CAGE, I CANNOT GET AT IT - IF I TEAR, IF I REND THE SLIGHT PRISON, MY OUTRAGE WILL ONLY LET THE CAPTIVE LOOSE.

CONQUEROR I MIGHT BE OF THE HOUSE, BUT THE INMATE WOULD ESCAPE TO HEAVEN BEFORE I COULD CALL MYSELF POSSESSOR OF ITS CLAY DWELLING PLACE.

AND IT IS YOU, SPIRIT - WITH WILL AND ENERGY, VIRTUE AND PURITY - THAT I WANT: NOT ALONE YOUR BRITTLE FRAME.

OF YOURSELF YOU COULD COME WITH SOFT FLIGHT AND NESTLE AGAINST MY HEART.

SEIZED AGAINST YOUR WILL, YOU WILL ELUDE THE GRASP LIKE AN ESSENCE - YOU WILL VANISH ERE I INHALE YOUR FRAGRANCE.

I AM **GOING**, SIR.

YOU ARE **LEAVING** ME?

YES. **GOD BLESS** YOU, MY **DEAR MASTER**!

AND **KEEP** YOU FROM **HARM** AND **WRONG** - **DIRECT** YOU, **SOLACE** YOU - **REWARD** YOU **WELL** FOR YOUR **PAST KINDNESS** TO ME. **FAREWELL**!

OH, **JANE**! MY **HOPE** - MY **LOVE** - MY **LIFE**!

I **ROSE** AT **DAWN** TO LEAVE THORNFIELD HALL. IN MR. ROCHESTER'S CHAMBER, THE **INMATE** WAS **WALKING RESTLESSLY** FROM **WALL** TO **WALL**. I **KNEW** WHAT I HAD TO **DO**, AND DID IT **MECHANICALLY**.

I WAS **OUT** OF **THORNFIELD**. THERE LAY A **ROAD** WHICH **STRETCHED** IN THE **CONTRARY** DIRECTION TO **MILLCOTE**; THITHER I BENT MY **STEPS**.

I **THOUGHT** OF HIM NOW, IN HIS **ROOM**, HOPING I SHOULD SOON COME TO **SAY** I WOULD BE **HIS**. I **LONGED** TO BE HIS; IT WAS NOT **TOO LATE**. I **COULD** GO **BACK** AND BE HIS **REDEEMER**. **BIRDS** WERE FAITHFUL TO THEIR MATES; **BIRDS** WERE **EMBLEMS** OF **LOVE**. WHAT WAS **I**? I HAD **INJURED** - **WOUNDED** - LEFT MY **MASTER**. I WAS **HATEFUL** IN MY **OWN** EYES. STILL I **COULD** NOT TURN, NOR **RETRACE** ONE STEP.

I WAS **WEEPING WILDLY** AS I WALKED: **FAST, FAST** I WENT LIKE ONE **DELIRIOUS**.

WHERE ARE YOU **GOING**?

WHITCROSS - FOR **THIRTY SHILLINGS**, MISS.

I **ONLY** HAVE **TWENTY**.

WELL, I WILL **TRY** TO **MAKE** IT DO. GET **INSIDE**.

MAY **NO-ONE** EVER FEEL WHAT I THEN FELT! TO BE THE **INSTRUMENT** OF **EVIL** TO WHAT THEY **WHOLLY LOVE**.

91

~ CHAPTER ~
~ XXVIII ~

AFTER **TWO DAYS**, THE **COACHMAN** SET ME **DOWN** AT **WHITCROSS**. IT IS NO **TOWN**; BUT A **STONE PILLAR** SET UP WHERE **FOUR ROADS** MEET.

WHEN THE **COACH** WAS A **MILE OFF**, I DISCOVERED THAT MY PARCEL REMAINED ON THE **COACH**. I WAS **ALONE** AND **DESTITUTE**. NOT A **TIE** HELD ME TO **HUMAN SOCIETY**. I HAD NO **RELATIVE** BUT THE **UNIVERSAL** MOTHER, **NATURE**.

NATURE SEEMED TO **ME BENIGN** AND **GOOD**; I THOUGHT SHE **LOVED ME**, OUTCAST AS I **WAS**; AND I, WHO FROM **MAN** COULD ANTICIPATE ONLY **MISTRUST, REJECTION, INSULT, CLUNG** TO HER WITH **FILIAL FONDNESS**.

TO-NIGHT, AT **LEAST**, I WOULD BE HER **GUEST**, AS I WAS HER **CHILD**. MY **REST** MIGHT HAVE BEEN **BLISSFUL ENOUGH**, ONLY A **SAD HEART BROKE** IT. IT **TREMBLED** FOR MR. **ROCHESTER** AND HIS **DOOM**; IT **DEMANDED** HIM WITH **CEASELESS LONGING**.

WE **KNOW** THAT **GOD** IS **EVERYWHERE**; WE **FEEL** HIS **PRESENCE MOST** WHEN HIS **WORKS** ARE ON THE **GRANDEST SCALE** SPREAD **BEFORE** US.

MR. **ROCHESTER** WAS **SAFE**: HE WAS **GOD'S**, AND BY **GOD** WOULD HE BE **GUARDED**.

BUT NEXT DAY, **WANT** CAME TO ME, PALE AND BARE. I TURNED TOWARDS A **CHURCH BELL** AND CAME ACROSS A NEARBY **HAMLET**. THERE I SOUGHT **EMPLOYMENT** BUT **FOUND NONE**. I SOUGHT **FOOD**, AND SHAMEFULLY OFFERED MY **POSSESSIONS** IN **EXCHANGE** – BUT WAS **REFUSED**.

ALL **DAY** I BEGGED AND **PRAYED** FOR PROVIDENCE.

DECIDING I WOULD RATHER **DIE** IN THE **LANDSCAPE** THAN IN THE **STREET**, I TURNED TOWARDS A HILL. AS NIGHT APPROACHED, I FOUND MYSELF **WALKING, EXHAUSTED**, TOWARDS A **DISTANT LIGHT**.

THIS **LIGHT** WAS MY **FORLORN HOPE**: I MUST **GAIN** IT.

I NEED A **NIGHT'S SHELTER** IN AN **OUTHOUSE** OR **ANYWHERE**, AND A **MORSEL** OF **BREAD** TO EAT.

I'LL GIVE YOU A PIECE OF **BREAD**, BUT WE **CAN'T** TAKE IN A **VAGRANT**.

BUT I MUST **DIE** IF I'M **TURNED AWAY**.

NOT YOU. I'M **FEAR'D** YOU HAVE SOME **ILL PLANS** AGATE, THAT **BRING YOU** ABOUT **FOLK'S HOUSES** AT **THIS** TIME O' NIGHT. WE HAVE A **GENTLEMAN** IN THE HOUSE, AND **DOGS**, AND **GUNS**.

I CAN BUT **DIE**, AND I **BELIEVE** IN **GOD**. LET ME **TRY** TO **WAIT** HIS **WILL** IN **SILENCE**.

ALL MEN MUST **DIE**. BUT **ALL** ARE **NOT CONDEMNED** TO MEET A **LINGERING**, **PREMATURE** DOOM, SUCH AS **YOURS** WOULD BE IF YOU **PERISHED** HERE OF **WANT**.

WHO OR **WHAT** SPEAKS?

IS IT **YOU**, MR. **ST. JOHN?** YOUR **SISTERS** ARE QUITE UNEASY. **BAD FOLKS** ARE ABOUT. A **BEGGAR-WOMAN** --

-- I DECLARE, SHE IS **NOT GONE YET!**

MOVE OFF, I SAY!

HUSH, HANNAH!

YOU HAVE **DONE YOUR DUTY** IN **EXCLUDING**, LET ME DO MINE IN **ADMITTING** HER. THIS IS A **PECULIAR CASE**.

THE **RECOLLECTION** OF ABOUT **THREE DAYS** AND NIGHTS **SUCCEEDING** THIS ARE VERY **DIM** IN MY MIND. THEY GAVE ME **FOOD**; I THEN LAY **MOTIONLESS** ON A **NARROW BED** IN A **SMALL** ROOM.

IT IS **VERY WELL** WE **TOOK HER IN**.

YES; SHE WOULD **CERTAINLY** HAVE BEEN FOUND **DEAD** AT THE **DOOR** IN THE **MORNING**. SHE IS NOT AN **UNEDUCATED** PERSON.

~ CHAPTER XXIX ~

ON THE **FIFTH DAY**, I WAS **WELL** ENOUGH TO **GET UP**. I **TOLD** THEM MY **NAME** WAS **JANE ELLIOTT**.

I **TRUST** I SHALL NOT **EAT** LONG AT YOUR **EXPENSE**.

NO, WHEN YOU TELL MY **SISTERS**, **DIANA** AND **MARY**, AND I YOUR **RESIDENCE**.

THAT IS **OUT** OF MY **POWER** TO DO, BEING **ABSOLUTELY** WITHOUT **HOME** AND **FRIENDS**.

A MOST **SINGULAR POSITION** AT **YOUR AGE!** YOU ARE A **SPINSTER?**

~ CHAPTER XXX ~

WHILE MY **HEALTH** RECOVERED, I JOINED **DIANA** AND **MARY** IN ALL THEIR **OCCUPATIONS** AND FOUND **BETWEEN** US A PERFECT **CONGENIALITY** OF **TASTES, SENTIMENTS,** AND **PRINCIPLES;** AND A CHARM BOTH **POTENT** AND PERMANENT IN THEIR **SEQUESTERED HOME** IN THE **PURPLE MOORS.**

THEY WERE BOTH **MORE ACCOMPLISHED** AND **BETTER READ** THAN I WAS. I **DEVOURED** THE **BOOKS** THEY LENT ME; **THEN** IT WAS **FULL SATISFACTION** TO **DISCUSS** WITH THEM IN THE EVENING WHAT I HAD **PERUSED** DURING THE **DAY.**

THOUGHT FITTED THOUGHT, **OPINION** MET OPINION. WE **COINCIDED,** IN **SHORT,** PERFECTLY.

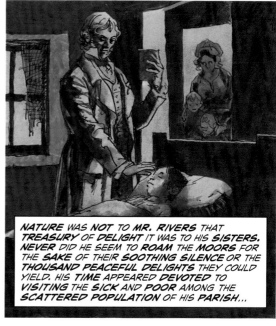

NATURE WAS **NOT** TO **MR. RIVERS** THAT **TREASURY** OF **DELIGHT** IT WAS TO HIS **SISTERS.** NEVER DID HE SEEM TO **ROAM** THE MOORS FOR THE **SAKE** OF THEIR **SOOTHING SILENCE** OR THE **THOUSAND PEACEFUL DELIGHTS** THEY COULD **YIELD. HIS TIME** APPEARED **DEVOTED** TO **VISITING** THE **SICK** AND **POOR** AMONG THE **SCATTERED POPULATION** OF HIS **PARISH,...**

...AND **PREACHING** IN HIS **OWN CHURCH.** WHEN HE HAD **FINISHED,** INSTEAD OF FEELING **BETTER,** I EXPERIENCED **SADNESS.** HE HAD NO MORE FOUND 'THE **PEACE** OF GOD WHICH PASSETH ALL **UNDERSTANDING'** THAN HAD I CONCEALED MY **REGRETS** FOR MY **BROKEN IDOL** AND **LOST ELYSIUM.**

MARY AND **DIANA** WILL SOON **LEAVE** MOOR HOUSE, AND **RETURN** AS GOVERNESSES TO **HAUGHTY FAMILIES** WHO NEITHER **KNOW** NOR **SEEK** THEIR **INNATE EXCELLENCES,** APPRECIATING THEM **ONLY** AS THEY APPRECIATE THE **SKILL** OF THEIR **COOK** OR THE **TASTE** OF THEIR **WAITING-WOMAN.**

MR. ST. JOHN HAD SAID NOTHING TO ME YET ABOUT THE EMPLOYMENT HE HAD PROMISED TO OBTAIN FOR ME. ONE MORNING, WE WERE ALONE IN THE PARLOUR...

I BELIEVE YOU WILL ACCEPT THE POST I OFFER YOU.

I MEAN TO OPEN A SCHOOL FOR GIRLS - WILL YOU BE ITS MISTRESS?

I THANK YOU FOR THE PROPOSAL, MR. RIVERS --

-- AND I ACCEPT IT WITH ALL MY HEART.

IT IS A VILLAGE SCHOOL, WITH A HOUSE KINDLY PROVIDED BY A RICH HEIRESS, MISS OLIVER.

YOUR SCHOLARS WILL BE ONLY POOR GIRLS. KNITTING, SEWING, READING, WRITING, CIPHERING, WILL BE ALL YOU WILL HAVE TO TEACH.

WHAT WILL YOU DO WITH YOUR ACCOMPLISHMENTS?

SAVE THEM TILL THEY ARE WANTED. THEY WILL KEEP. I WILL OPEN THE SCHOOL NEXT WEEK, IF YOU LIKE.

VERY WELL: SO BE IT.

YOU WILL NOT STAY LONG; I READ IT IN YOUR EYE.

I AM NOT AMBITIOUS.

WELL IF YOU ARE NOT AMBITIOUS, YOU ARE --

-- IMPASSIONED...

...HUMAN AFFECTION AND SYMPATHIES HAVE A MOST POWERFUL HOLD ON YOU. I AM SURE YOU CANNOT DEVOTE YOUR WORKING HOURS TO A MONOTONOUS LABOUR WHOLLY VOID OF STIMULUS, ANY MORE THAN I.

A MISSIONARY I RESOLVE TO BE.

YOU HEAR NOW HOW I CONTRADICT MYSELF. I, WHO PREACH CONTENTMENT WITH A HUMBLE LOT, ALMOST RAVE IN MY RESTLESSNESS.

IN THIS BRIEF HOUR I HAD LEARNT MORE OF HIM THAN IN THE WHOLE PREVIOUS MONTH: YET STILL HE PUZZLED ME.

ST. JOHN WILL SACRIFICE **ALL** TO HIS **LONG-FRAMED RESOLVES**. HE **LOOKS** QUIET, JANE; BUT HE **HIDES** A FEVER IN HIS **VITALS**. YOU WOULD **THINK** HIM **GENTLE**, YET IN **SOME** THINGS HE IS **INEXORABLE** AS DEATH.

IT IS **RIGHT**, **NOBLE**, CHRISTIAN: YET IT **BREAKS** MY **HEART**!

WE ARE NOW WITHOUT **FATHER**. WE SHALL **SOON** BE WITHOUT **HOME** AND **BROTHER**.

AT **THAT MOMENT** A **LITTLE ACCIDENT** SUPERVENED, WHICH **SEEMED** TO PROVE THAT **MISFORTUNES** NEVER COME **SINGLY**.

OUR **UNCLE JOHN** IS **DEAD**.

AND WHAT **THEN?**

WHAT **THEN?** WHY - **NOTHING**.

READ.

AT **ANY** RATE, IT MAKES US NO **WORSE** OFF THAN WE WERE **BEFORE**.

WE HAVE **NEVER SEEN** OUR **UNCLE**.

LONG **AGO**, HE GAVE MY **FATHER** SOME **BAD BUSINESS** ADVICE WHICH **RUINED** HIM.

AFTERWARDS, MY **UNCLE** REALISED A **FORTUNE** AND MY **FATHER** CHERISHED THE **IDEA** THAT HE WOULD **ATONE** BY LEAVING HIS **POSSESSIONS** TO **US**.

HE HAS **NOT**.

WE WOULD HAVE **ESTEEMED** OURSELVES **RICH**, AND IT **WOULD** HAVE ENABLED ST. **JOHN** TO DO **MUCH GOOD**.

IN A **WEEK**, THE **OLD GRANGE** WAS **ABANDONED**. THE **VILLAGE SCHOOL** OPENED WITH **TWENTY SCHOLARS**. SOME WERE **UNMANNERED**, **ROUGH**, **INTRACTABLE**, AS WELL AS **IGNORANT**; BUT **OTHERS** WERE **DOCILE**, HAD A **WISH** TO **LEARN**, AND **PLEASING DISPOSITIONS**.

~ CHAPTER XXXI ~

BUT **THREE** OF THE **NUMBER** CAN **READ**: NONE **WRITE** OR **CIPHER**. SEVERAL **KNIT**, AND A FEW **SEW** A LITTLE.

WHICH IS **BETTER?** TO HAVE **SURRENDERED** TO TEMPTATION; LISTENED TO PASSION; - BUT TO HAVE **SUNK DOWN** IN THE **SILKEN SNARE,** FEVERED WITH **DELUSIVE BLISS** ONE HOUR, **SUFFOCATING** WITH TEARS OF **REMORSE** AND **SHAME** THE **NEXT?**

OR TO BE A **VILLAGE SCHOOL-MISTRESS,** FREE AND HONEST, IN A **BREEZY NOOK** IN THE **HEALTHY HEART** OF **ENGLAND?**

THE **BIRDS SANG** THEIR **LAST STRAINS** OF THE **DAY.** I THOUGHT MYSELF **HAPPY,** AND WAS **SURPRISED** TO FIND MYSELF ERE **LONG** WEEPING FOR WHAT I HAD **LEFT BEHIND.**

I **CANNOT STAY.** I HAVE ONLY BROUGHT YOU A LITTLE **PARCEL** MY **SISTERS** LEFT FOR YOU.

I **THINK** IT CONTAINS A **COLOUR-BOX, PENCILS,** AND **PAPER.**

A **WELCOME GIFT.**

DO YOU FIND **SOLITUDE** AN **OPPRESSION?**

I HAVE **HARDLY** HAD **TIME YET** TO ENJOY A SENSE OF **TRANQUILLITY,** MUCH LESS **LONELINESS.**

IT IS **HARD WORK** TO **CONTROL** THE WORKINGS OF **INCLINATION** AND **TURN** THE **BENT** OF **NATURE;** BUT THAT IT **MAY BE DONE,** I KNOW FROM **EXPERIENCE.**

GOOD-EVENING, MR. RIVERS. YOUR **DOG** IS **QUICKER** TO **RECOGNISE** HIS **FRIENDS** THAN **YOU ARE,** SIR.

THIS THEN, I THOUGHT, IS **MISS ROSAMOND OLIVER,** THE **HEIRESS.**

A **LOVELY EVENING,** BUT **LATE** FOR YOU TO BE **OUT ALONE.**

PAPA TOLD ME YOU HAD **OPENED** YOUR **SCHOOL,** AND THAT THE NEW **MISTRESS** WAS COME; **THIS** IS **SHE?**

IT **IS.**

I SHALL **COME UP** AND **HELP TEACH** SOMETIMES. IT WILL BE A **CHANGE** FOR ME TO **VISIT** NOW AND AGAIN; AND I **LIKE** A **CHANGE.**

PAPA SAYS YOU **NEVER** COME TO **SEE US** NOW. YOU ARE **QUITE** A **STRANGER** AT **VALE HALL.**

DO COME AND SEE **PAPA.**

NOT TO-NIGHT, MISS ROSAMOND.

SHE WENT **ONE WAY;** HE ANOTHER.

THIS **SPECTACLE** OF **ANOTHER'S SUFFERING** AND **SACRIFICE** RAPT MY **THOUGHTS** FROM **EXCLUSIVE MEDITATION** ON MY **OWN.** DIANA RIVERS HAD **DESIGNATED** HER BROTHER "**INEXORABLE AS DEATH**". SHE HAD **NOT EXAGGERATED.**

I FELT I BECAME A **FAVOURITE** IN THE NEIGHBOURHOOD. TO **LIVE** AMIDST **GENERAL REGARD** IS LIKE 'SITTING IN SUNSHINE, CALM AND **SWEET**'; SERENE INWARD FEELINGS **BUD** AND **BLOOM** UNDER THE **RAY**. AT THIS PERIOD, MY **HEART** FAR MORE OFTENER **SWELLED** WITH **THANKFULNESS** THAN SANK WITH **DEJECTION**.

ROSAMOND HAD A **POWER** OVER **MR. RIVERS**. HER **EYE** PIERCES THE YOUNG PASTOR'S **HEART**. INDEED, HE **COULD NOT CONCEAL** HIS **RESPONSE**. HE SEEMED TO **SAY**, WITH HIS **SAD**, **RESOLUTE** LOOK, "I **LOVE YOU** AND I **KNOW** YOU **PREFER** ME, BUT MY **HEART** IS **ALREADY LAID** ON A **SACRED ALTAR**. IT WILL **SOON BE NO MORE** THAN A **SACRIFICE CONSUMED**."

~ CHAPTER XXXII ~

I AM **COME** TO **SEE** HOW YOU ARE **SPENDING** YOUR **HOLIDAY**.

I HAVE **BROUGHT YOU** A **BOOK** FOR **EVENING SOLACE**.

IS THIS **PORTRAIT LIKE**?

LIKE **WHOM**? I DID NOT **OBSERVE** IT **CLOSELY**.

YOU **DID**, MR. RIVERS. WHO IS IT **LIKE**?

MISS **OLIVER**, I **PRESUME**.

TO **REWARD** YOU FOR THE **ACCURATE** GUESS, I WILL **PROMISE** TO **PAINT YOU** A **DUPLICATE**.

WOULD IT **COMFORT**, OR WOULD IT **WOUND YOU** TO **HAVE** IT?

THAT I SHOULD **LIKE** TO **HAVE** IT IS **CERTAIN**: WHETHER IT WOULD BE **JUDICIOUS** OR **WISE** IS **ANOTHER** QUESTION.

SHE **LIKES** YOU, I AM **SURE**.

DOES SHE LIKE ME?

CERTAINLY; **BETTER** THAN SHE LIKES **ANYONE ELSE**.

SHE **TALKS** OF YOU **CONTINUALLY**: THERE IS **NO SUBJECT** SHE **ENJOYS** SO MUCH OR **TOUCHES** UPON SO **OFTEN**.

IT IS VERY **PLEASANT** TO **HEAR** THIS. **VERY**: GO ON FOR ANOTHER **QUARTER** OF AN **HOUR**.

BUT **WHERE** IS THE **USE** OF **GOING ON**, WHEN YOU ARE **PROBABLY** FORGING A **FRESH CHAIN** TO FETTER YOUR **HEART**?

DON'T **IMAGINE** SUCH **HARD** THINGS. SHE IS **TALKING** TO ME WITH HER **SWEET VOICE**, **SMILING** AT ME WITH THESE **CORAL** LIPS. SHE IS **MINE** - I AM **HERS**

HUSH! SAY **NOTHING** - MY **HEART** IS FULL OF **DELIGHT** - MY **SENSES** ARE **ENTRANCED** - LET THE **TIME** I **MARKED** PASS IN **PEACE**.

NOW, THAT **LITTLE** SPACE WAS **GIVEN** TO **DELIRIUM** AND **DELUSION**. I **RESTED** MY **TEMPLES** ON THE **BREAST** OF **TEMPTATION**.

HER **PROMISES** ARE **HOLLOW** - HER **OFFERS FALSE**.

IT IS **STRANGE** THAT WHILE I **LOVE** ROSAMOND OLIVER SO **WILDLY**, I **KNOW** THAT SHE WOULD **NOT** MAKE ME A **GOOD WIFE**; SHE IS **NOT** THE **PARTNER SUITED** TO ME.

TWELVE MONTHS' **RAPTURE** WOULD **SUCCEED** A **LIFETIME** OF **REGRET**.

STRANGE, INDEED!

SHE IS **LOVELY**. SHE IS **WELL NAMED** THE **ROSE OF THE WORLD**, INDEED!

AND MAY I NOT **PAINT** ONE **LIKE** IT FOR **YOU**?

CUI BONO?

NO.

WHAT IS THE **MATTER**?

NOTHING IN THE **WORLD**. GOOD-**AFTERNOON**.

WELL! THAT **CAPS** THE **GLOBE!**

I SAW HIM **TEAR** A NARROW SLIP FROM THE **MARGIN**; AND, WITH ONE **HASTY** NOD, HE **VANISHED**.

100

WHEN MR. ST. JOHN WENT, IT WAS *BEGINNING TO SNOW*; THE WHIRLING *STORM* CONTINUED *ALL NIGHT.* THE NEXT DAY, A *KEEN WIND* BROUGHT *FRESH* AND *BLINDING* FALLS; BY TWILIGHT THE *VALLEY* WAS ALMOST *IMPASSABLE.* I HEARD A *NOISE*: THE WIND, I THOUGHT, SHOOK THE *DOOR.* NO; IT WAS *ST. JOHN RIVERS.*

ANY *ILL NEWS*? HAS ANYTHING *HAPPENED*? WHY ARE YOU *COME*?

RATHER AN *INHOSPITABLE QUESTION*: BUT SINCE YOU *ASK IT*, I *ANSWER* SIMPLY TO HAVE A *LITTLE TALK* WITH YOU.

~ CHAPTER ~
~ XXXIII ~

I GOT *TIRED* OF MY *MUTE BOOKS* AND *EMPTY ROOMS.* BESIDES, SINCE *YESTERDAY* I HAVE EXPERIENCED THE *EXCITEMENT* OF A *PERSON* TO WHOM A *TALE* HAS BEEN *HALF-TOLD*, AND WHO IS *IMPATIENT* TO HEAR THE *SEQUEL.*

I *BEGAN* TO FEAR HIS *WITS* WERE *TOUCHED.* HE *SAT* FOR HALF AN HOUR, SAYING *LITTLE*: HIS EYE DWELLING *DREAMILY* ON THE GLOWING *GRATE.* THEN...

IT IS *FAIR* TO *WARN YOU* THAT THIS *STORY* WILL SOUND SOMEWHAT *HACKNEYED* IN YOUR *EARS. STALE DETAILS* OFTEN *REGAIN* A DEGREE OF *FRESHNESS* WHEN THEY *PASS* THROUGH *NEW LIPS.*

TWENTY YEARS *AGO*, A *POOR CURATE* - NEVER *MIND* HIS *NAME* AT THE MOMENT - FELL IN *LOVE* WITH A *RICH MAN'S DAUGHTER.* SHE *MARRIED HIM* AGAINST THE *ADVICE* OF HER *FRIENDS*, WHO CONSEQUENTLY *DISOWNED* HER IMMEDIATELY AFTER THE *WEDDING.*

BEFORE *TWO YEARS* PASSED, THE *RASH PAIR* WERE BOTH *DEAD.* I HAVE *SEEN* THEIR *GRAVE.*

THEY LEFT A *DAUGHTER. CHARITY* CARRIED THE *FRIENDLESS THING* TO THE *HOUSE* OF ITS *RICH MATERNAL RELATIONS.* IT WAS *REARED* BY AN *AUNT*-IN-LAW CALLED - I COME TO *NAMES* NOW -

MRS. REED OF GATESHEAD.

=GASP!=

YOU *START.* DID YOU HEAR A *NOISE*?

HE *WENT ON* WITH THE *REST* OF MY *OWN HISTORY.*

...SHE *LEFT LOWOOD SCHOOL* TO BE A *GOVERNESS.* THERE, AGAIN, YOUR *FATES* ARE *ANALOGOUS.* SHE *UNDERTOOK* THE *EDUCATION* OF THE *WARD* OF A CERTAIN *MR. ROCHESTER* --

MR. RIVERS!

-- I CAN *GUESS* YOUR *FEELINGS*, BUT *RESTRAIN* THEM FOR A WHILE.

I *HEARD* THE *STORY* OF MY *WEDDING-DAY.*

...THIS YOUNG GIRL HAD **LEFT** THORNFIELD HALL IN THE **NIGHT**. EVERY **RESEARCH** AFTER HER **COURSE** HAD BEEN IN **VAIN**.

YET THAT SHE SHOULD BE **FOUND** IS BECOME A **MATTER** OF **SERIOUS URGENCY**.

ADVERTISEMENTS HAVE BEEN PUT IN **ALL** THE **PAPERS**.

I **RECEIVED** THESE DETAILS IN A **LETTER** FROM A **SOLICITOR** CALLED **MR. BRIGGS**.

HE TALKS OF A **JANE EYRE**: I KNEW A **JANE ELLIOTT**.

YESTERDAY, MY **SUSPICIONS** WERE AT **ONCE** RESOLVED INTO **CERTAINTY**.

MY **SIGNATURE** FROM THE **PORTRAIT**.

MR. **BRIGGS** SOUGHT **AFTER** YOU TO **TELL** YOU THAT YOUR **UNCLE**, MR. **EYRE** OF MADEIRA, IS **DEAD**; THAT HE HAS **LEFT** YOU **ALL** HIS **PROPERTY**, AND THAT **YOU** ARE NOW **RICH** -

MERELY THAT - **NOTHING** MORE.

I! - **RICH**? HOW **MUCH** AM I **WORTH**?

TWENTY THOUSAND POUNDS.

WELL - IF YOU HAD COMMITTED A **MURDER**, AND I HAD **TOLD YOU** YOUR **CRIME** WAS **DISCOVERED**, YOU COULD **SCARCELY** LOOK MORE **AGHAST**.

IT **PUZZLES** ME TO **KNOW** WHY MR. **BRIGGS WROTE** TO YOU ABOUT ME.

OH, THE CLERGY ARE **OFTEN** APPEALED TO ABOUT **ODD MATTERS**.

NO; THAT DOES NOT **SATISFY** ME! I **MUST** KNOW **MORE** ABOUT IT.

YOU ARE **NOT**, PERHAPS, **AWARE** THAT I AM YOUR **NAMESAKE**? - THAT I WAS **CHRISTENED** ST. JOHN **EYRE** RIVERS?

NO, INDEED! I **REMEMBER** NOW SEEING YOUR **INITIAL 'E'** WRITTEN IN **BOOKS** YOU HAVE LENT ME.

MY **MOTHER'S** NAME WAS **EYRE**. SHE HAD **TWO** BROTHERS; ONE A **CLERGYMAN**, WHO MARRIED **MISS JANE REED**, OF **GATESHEAD** --

-- THE **OTHER**, **JOHN EYRE**, **ESQ.**, **MERCHANT**, LATE OF **FUNCHAL**, **MADEIRA**.

UNCLE JOHN LEFT HIS **PROPERTY** TO HIS **BROTHER** THE **CLERGYMAN'S** ORPHAN DAUGHTER, OVERLOOKING US IN CONSEQUENCE OF A **QUARREL**, NEVER **FORGIVEN**.

YOUR **MOTHER** WAS MY **FATHER'S SISTER**? MY **UNCLE JOHN** WAS **YOUR UNCLE JOHN**?

YOU, DIANA AND **MARY**, THEN, ARE MY **COUSINS**.

WE ARE **COUSINS**; YES.

THIS WAS **WEALTH INDEED**! WEALTH TO THE **HEART**! THIS WAS A **BLESSING** AND **EXHILARATING**; NOT LIKE THE **PONDEROUS GIFT** OF **GOLD**.

OH, I AM GLAD! - **I AM GLAD!**

YOU WERE **SERIOUS** WHEN I TOLD YOU YOU HAD GOT A **FORTUNE**; AND **NOW**, FOR A **MATTER** OF **NO MOMENT**, YOU ARE **EXCITED**.

WHAT **CAN** YOU **MEAN**? IT **MAY** BE OF **NO MOMENT** TO **YOU**; YOU HAVE **SISTERS**; BUT I HAD **NOBODY**; AND NOW **THREE** RELATIONS ARE BORN INTO MY WORLD **FULL-GROWN**. I SAY **AGAIN**, I AM **GLAD**!

THOSE WHO HAD **SAVED** MY **LIFE**, I COULD NOW **BENEFIT**. THEY WERE UNDER A **YOKE** - I COULD **FREE** THEM:

THE **INDEPENDENCE**, THE **AFFLUENCE** WHICH WAS **MINE**, MIGHT BE **THEIRS** TOO. WERE WE NOT **FOUR**? **FIVE THOUSAND POUNDS EACH**.

WRITE TO **DIANA** AND **MARY** AND TELL THEM TO **COME HOME DIRECTLY** FOR THE **FORTUNE** THAT HAS **ACCRUED** TO THEM.

TO **YOU**, YOU MEAN.

JANE, I WILL BE YOUR **BROTHER** - MY **SISTERS** WILL BE **YOUR** SISTERS - **WITHOUT** THIS **SACRIFICE** OF YOUR **JUST RIGHTS**.

I, **WEALTHY** - **GORGED** WITH **GOLD** I NEVER **EARNED** AND DO NOT **MERIT**!

YOU, **PENNILESS**?!

AND THE **SCHOOL**, **MISS EYRE**? IT MUST **NOW** BE **SHUT UP**, I SUPPOSE?

NO, I WILL **RETAIN** MY POST OF MISTRESS TILL YOU FIND A **SUBSTITUTE**.

I WAS **ABSOLUTELY RESOLVED**. THE **INSTRUMENTS** OF **TRANSFER** WERE DRAWN OUT: **ST. JOHN, DIANA, MARY**, AND I, EACH BECAME **POSSESSED** OF A **COMPETENCY**.

IT WAS **NEAR CHRISTMAS** BY THE TIME **ALL** WAS SETTLED. I NOW **CLOSED** MORTON SCHOOL. HANNAH, ST. JOHN'S **SERVANT**, **HELPED** ME TO PUT **EVERYTHING** IN ORDER AT **MOOR HOUSE** READY FOR DIANA AND MARY'S **ARRIVAL**.

I **TRUST** WHEN THIS IS **OVER**, YOU WILL **LOOK** A LITTLE **HIGHER** THAN DOMESTIC **ENDEARMENTS** AND **HOUSEHOLD JOYS**.

THE **BEST THINGS** THE **WORLD** HAS!

NO, JANE, **NO**: **THIS** WORLD IS NOT THE SCENE OF **FRUITION**; DO NOT **ATTEMPT** TO **MAKE** IT SO.

ST. JOHN, I **THINK** YOU ARE **ALMOST WICKED** TO TALK SO. I AM **DISPOSED** TO BE AS **CONTENT** AS A **QUEEN**, AND YOU TRY TO **STIR** ME UP TO **RESTLESSNESS!** TO WHAT END?

TO THE **END** OF TURNING TO **PROFIT** THE **TALENTS** WHICH **GOD** HAS COMMITTED TO YOUR **KEEPING**.

DON'T CLING SO **TENACIOUSLY** TO TIES OF THE **FLESH**.

EVERYTHING WAS **ARRANGED** WITH **MATHEMATICAL PRECISION**. ENOUGH **COAL** AND **PEAT** WERE STOCKED TO KEEP UP **GOOD FIRES** IN **EVERY ROOM**. THE **LAST** TWO DAYS, HANNAH AND I BAKED **CHRISTMAS CAKES** AND **MINCE PIES**. WHEN ALL WAS **FINISHED**, I THOUGHT **MOOR HOUSE** AS COMPLETE A MODEL OF **BRIGHT MODEST SNUGNESS WITHIN**, AS IT WAS A **SPECIMEN** OF **WINTRY WASTE WITHOUT**.

THE **EVENTFUL THURSDAY** AT LENGTH **CAME**. THEY WERE **EXPECTED** ABOUT **DARK**. ST. JOHN ARRIVED FIRST.

ARE YOU **AT LAST** SATISFIED WITH **HOUSEMAID'S WORK?**

PLEASE ACCOMPANY ME ON A **GENERAL INSPECTION**.

NOT A **SYLLABLE** DID HE **UTTER** INDICATING **PLEASURE** IN THE **IMPROVED ASPECT** OF HIS **ABODE**.

THE **SILENCE DAMPED** ME. I COMPREHENDED ALL AT **ONCE** THAT IT WOULD BE A **TRYING THING** TO BE HIS **WIFE**.

ST. JOHN, ARE YOUR PLANS YET UNCHANGED?

UNCHANGED AND UNCHANGEABLE. MY DEPARTURE FROM ENGLAND IS NOW FIXED FOR THE ENSUING YEAR.

AND ROSAMOND OLIVER?

ROSAMOND IS ABOUT TO BE MARRIED TO MR. GRANBY: A WELL-CONNECTED AND MOST ESTIMABLE PERSONAGE, AND GRANDSON AND HEIR TO SIR FREDERIC GRANBY.

THE MATCH MUST HAVE BEEN GOT UP HASTILY. THEY CANNOT HAVE KNOWN EACH OTHER LONG.

BUT TWO MONTHS. THEY MET IN OCTOBER AT THE COUNTY BALL. BUT WHERE THERE ARE NO OBSTACLES TO A UNION, WHERE THE CONNECTION IS IN EVERY POINT DESIRABLE, DELAYS ARE UNNECESSARY.

JANE, WHAT ARE YOU DOING?

LEARNING GERMAN.

I WANT YOU TO GIVE UP GERMAN AND LEARN HINDOSTANEE. IT IS THE LANGUAGE I AM STUDYING. WOULD YOU HELP ME UNTIL I DEPART IN THREE MONTHS' TIME?

IF YOU ARE IN EARNEST.

IN SUCH EARNEST THAT I MUST HAVE IT SO.

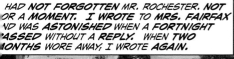

HAD NOT FORGOTTEN MR. ROCHESTER. NOT FOR A MOMENT. I WROTE TO MRS. FAIRFAX AND WAS ASTONISHED WHEN A FORTNIGHT PASSED WITHOUT A REPLY. WHEN TWO MONTHS WORE AWAY, I WROTE AGAIN.

WHEN HALF A YEAR WASTED IN VAIN EXPECTANCY, MY HOPE DIED OUT, AND THEN I FELT DARK INDEED.

BY DEGREES, ST. JOHN ACQUIRED A CERTAIN INFLUENCE OVER ME THAT TOOK AWAY MY LIBERTY OF MIND. I DAILY WISHED MORE TO PLEASE HIM; BUT TO DO SO, I FELT THAT I MUST DISOWN HALF MY NATURE.

JANE, COME WITH ME TO INDIA.

GOD AND NATURE INTENDED YOU FOR A MISSIONARY'S WIFE. YOU ARE FORMED FOR LABOUR, NOT FOR LOVE.

A MISSIONARY'S WIFE YOU MUST - SHALL BE.

YOU SHALL BE MINE: I CLAIM YOU - NOT FOR MY PLEASURE, BUT FOR MY SOVEREIGN'S SERVICE.

ALAS! IF I JOIN ST. JOHN, I ABANDON HALF MYSELF.

I WANT A WIFE: THE SOLE HELPMEET I CAN INFLUENCE EFFICIENTLY IN LIFE, AND RETAIN ABSOLUTELY TILL DEATH.

I AM READY TO GO TO INDIA, IF I MAY GO FREE.

YOUR ANSWER REQUIRES A COMMENTARY. IT IS NOT CLEAR.

SEEK A WIFE ELSEWHERE THAN IN ME.

I WILL GIVE THE MISSIONARY MY ENERGIES, BUT NOT MYSELF.

DO YOU THINK GOD WILL BE SATISFIED WITH HALF AN OBLIGATION? I CANNOT ACCEPT ON HIS BEHALF A DIVIDED ALLEGIANCE.

IT MUST BE ENTIRE.

OH! I WILL GIVE MY HEART TO GOD.

YOU DO NOT WANT IT.

WE MUST BE MARRIED; AND UNDOUBTEDLY ENOUGH OF LOVE WOULD FOLLOW UPON MARRIAGE TO RENDER THE UNION RIGHT EVEN IN YOUR EYES.

I SCORN YOUR IDEA OF LOVE AND THE COUNTERFEIT SENTIMENT YOU OFFER:

YES, ST. JOHN, AND I SCORN YOU WHEN YOU OFFER IT.

I SCARCELY EXPECTED TO HEAR THAT EXPRESSION FROM YOU.

I HAVE DONE AND UTTERED NOTHING TO DESERVE SCORN.

FORGIVE ME THE WORDS; BUT YOU INTRODUCED A TOPIC WE SHOULD NEVER DISCUSS. ABANDON YOUR SCHEME OF MARRIAGE.

IT IS A LONG-CHERISHED SCHEME; BUT I SHALL URGE YOU NO FURTHER AT PRESENT.

DO NOT FORGET THAT IF YOU REJECT IT, IT IS NOT ME YOU DENY; BUT GOD.

ST. JOHN MADE ME FEEL WHAT SEVERE PUNISHMENT A GOOD YET STERN MAN CAN INFLICT ON ONE WHO HAS OFFENDED HIM. WITHOUT ONE OVERT ACT OF HOSTILITY, HE CONTRIVED TO IMPRESS ME MOMENTLY WITH THE CONVICTION THAT I WAS PUT BEYOND THE PALE OF HIS FAVOUR. I FELT HOW, IF I WERE HIS WIFE, THIS GOOD MAN COULD SOON KILL ME, WITHOUT DRAWING FROM MY VEINS A SINGLE DROP OF BLOOD.

MUST WE PART IN THIS WAY, ST. JOHN?

WHEN YOU GO TO INDIA, WILL YOU LEAVE ME SO, WITHOUT A KINDER WORD THAN YOU HAVE YET SPOKEN?

WHAT! DO YOU NOT GO TO INDIA?

YOU SAID I COULD NOT UNLESS I MARRIED YOU.

AND YOU WILL NOT MARRY ME!

YOU ADHERE TO THAT RESOLUTION?

WHAT TERROR THOSE COLD PEOPLE CAN PUT INTO THE ICE OF THEIR QUESTIONS. HOW MUCH OF THE FALL OF THE AVALANCHE IS IN THEIR ANGER?

NO, ST. JOHN, I WILL NOT MARRY YOU.

THERE IS A POINT ON WHICH I HAVE LONG ENDURED PAINFUL DOUBT, AND I CAN GO NOWHERE TILL BY SOME MEANS THAT DOUBT IS REMOVED.

ARE YOU GOING TO SEEK MR. ROCHESTER?

I MUST FIND OUT WHAT IS BECOME OF HIM.

IT REMAINS FOR ME, THEN, TO REMEMBER YOU IN MY PRAYERS.

ST. JOHN WAS TO GO TO **CAMBRIDGE.** I TENDERED MY HAND, AND WISHED HIM A *PLEASANT JOURNEY.*

I STOOD **MOTIONLESS** UNDER MY **HIEROPHANT'S** TOUCH. MY **REFUSALS** WERE **FORGOTTEN.**

THE **IMPOSSIBLE** - MY **MARRIAGE** WITH **ST JOHN** - WAS **FAST** BECOMING THE **POSSIBLE.**

ALL WAS CHANGING UTTERLY WITH A **SUDDEN SWEEP.**

RELIGION CALLED - GOD COMMANDED.

THE **DIM ROOM** WAS **FULL** OF **VISIONS.**

LIFE

COULD YOU **DECIDE** NOW?

WERE I BUT **CONVINCED** THAT IT IS **GOD'S WILL** I **SHOULD** MARRY YOU, I COULD **VOW** TO MARRY YOU **HERE** AND **NOW!**

MY **PRAYERS** ARE **HEARD!**

I HEARD A **VOICE** SOMEWHERE **CRY.**

JANE! JANE! JANE!

O **GOD!** WHAT **IS** IT?

IT WAS THE **VOICE** OF A **HUMAN BEING** - A **KNOWN, LOVED, WELL-REMEMBERED** VOICE - THAT OF **EDWARD FAIRFAX ROCHESTER;** AND IT **SPOKE** IN PAIN AND **WOE,** WILDLY, EERILY, URGENTLY.

WHAT HAVE YOU **HEARD? WHAT** DO YOU **SEE?**

I AM **COMING!**

WAIT FOR ME!

OH, I WILL **COME!**

WHERE ARE YOU?

DOWN SUPERSTITION! THIS IS NOT THY DECEPTION, NOR THY WITCHCRAFT: IT IS THE WORK OF NATURE.

SHE WAS ROUSED, AND DID - NO MIRACLE - BUT HER BEST.

THE HILLS BEYOND MARSH GLEN SENT THE ANSWER FAINTLY BACK, "WHERE ARE YOU?" I LISTENED. THE WIND SIGHED LOW IN THE FIRS: ALL WAS MOORLAND LONELINESS AND MIDNIGHT HUSH.

~ CHAPTER ~
~ XXXVI ~

THE DAYLIGHT CAME. I ROSE AT DAWN. ST. JOHN PASSED A NOTE UNDER MY DOOR...

'YOU LEFT ME TOO SUDDENLY LAST NIGHT. HAD YOU BUT STAYED A LITTLE LONGER, YOU WOULD HAVE LAID YOUR HAND ON THE CHRISTIAN'S CROSS AND THE ANGEL'S CROWN. I SHALL EXPECT YOUR DECISION WHEN I RETURN FROM CAMBRIDGE.'

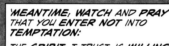

'MEANTIME, WATCH AND PRAY THAT YOU ENTER NOT INTO TEMPTATION:

THE SPIRIT, I TRUST, IS WILLING; BUT THE FLESH, I SEE, IS WEAK.

I SHALL PRAY FOR YOU HOURLY.

- YOURS,
ST. JOHN.'

MY SPIRIT IS WILLING TO DO WHAT IS RIGHT; WHEN ONCE THAT WILL IS DISTINCTLY KNOWN TO ME.

ERE MANY DAYS, I WILL KNOW SOMETHING OF HIM WHOSE VOICE SEEMED LAST NIGHT TO SUMMON ME. LETTERS HAVE PROVED OF NO AVAIL - PERSONAL INQUIRY SHALL REPLACE THEM.

I AM **GOING** ON A **JOURNEY** AND SHALL BE **ABSENT** AT **LEAST FOUR DAYS.**

ALONE, JANE?

YES; IT IS TO **SEE** OR **HEAR NEWS** OF A **FRIEND** ABOUT WHOM I **HAVE** FOR **SOME TIME** BEEN **UNEASY.**

WITH HER **TRUE NATURAL DELICACY,** SHE **ABSTAINED** FROM **COMMENT,** EXCEPT THAT SHE **ASKED** ME IF I WAS **SURE** I WAS **WELL ENOUGH** TO TRAVEL. I LOOKED VERY **PALE,** SHE **OBSERVED.** I REPLIED THAT **NOTHING** AILED ME SAVE **ANXIETY** OF **MIND,** WHICH I HOPED SOON TO **ALLEVIATE.**

IT WAS **EASY** TO MAKE MY **FURTHER** ARRANGEMENTS; FOR I WAS **TROUBLED** WITH NO **INQUIRIES** - NO **SURMISES.**

IT WAS A **JOURNEY** OF **SIX-AND-THIRTY** HOURS.

'THE **ROCHESTER ARMS'!** I AM **ALREADY** ON MY **MASTER'S** VERY **LANDS.**

ROCHESTER ARMS

I GAVE A **BOX** I HAD INTO THE **OSTLER'S CHARGE,** TO BE **KEPT** UNTIL I **CALLED** FOR IT...

...AND **HASTENED** ACROSS THE **FINAL TWO MILES** TO **THORNFIELD HALL.**

HOW I LOOKED FORWARD TO CATCH THE **FIRST VIEW** OF THE **WELL-KNOWN WOODS!** AT **LAST,** ITS **ROOKERY** CLUSTERED **DARK.** A **LOUD CAWING** OF **CROWS** BROKE THE **MORNING STILLNESS.**

WHO WOULD BE **HURT** BY MY **ONCE MORE** TASTING THE **LIFE** HIS **GLANCE** CAN **GIVE** ME?

I **RAVE:** PERHAPS HE IS **WATCHING** THE **SUN RISE** OVER THE **PYRENEES.**

I **LOOKED** WITH **TIMOROUS JOY** TOWARDS A **STATELY HOUSE...**

...I **SAW** A **BLACKENED RUIN.**

I RETURNED TO THE INN.

YOU **KNOW** THORNFIELD HALL, OF COURSE?

YES, MA'AM, I **LIVED** THERE ONCE.

I WAS THE **LATE** MR. ROCHESTER'S BUTLER.

=GASP!=

THE **LATE!** IS HE **DEAD?**

I MEAN THE **PRESENT** GENTLEMAN MR. EDWARD'S FATHER.

GLADDENING WORDS! MY MR. ROCHESTER WAS AT **LEAST** ALIVE.

I SUPPOSE YOU ARE A **STRANGER** IN THESE PARTS, OR YOU WOULD HAVE HEARD WHAT **HAPPENED** LAST AUTUMN.

THORNFIELD HALL WAS BURNT DOWN JUST ABOUT **HARVEST** TIME. THE **FIRE** BROKE OUT AT **DEAD OF NIGHT.**

AT **DEAD** OF **NIGHT!** WAS IT **KNOWN** HOW IT **ORIGINATED?**

THEY **GUESSED,** MA'AM.

YOU ARE NOT PERHAPS **AWARE** — THERE WAS A **LADY** — A **LUNATIC,** KEPT IN THE **HOUSE?**

I HAVE HEARD **SOMETHING** OF IT.

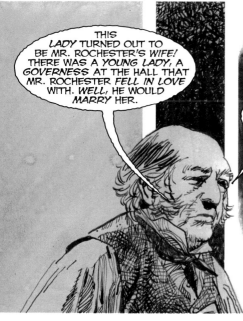

THIS **LADY** TURNED OUT TO BE MR. ROCHESTER'S **WIFE!** THERE WAS A **YOUNG LADY,** A GOVERNESS AT THE HALL THAT MR. ROCHESTER FELL IN LOVE WITH. **WELL,** HE WOULD **MARRY** HER.

HIS **LUNATIC** WIFE WAS TAKEN **CARE** OF BY A WOMAN CALLED MRS. **POOLE.**

MRS. POOLE HAD A COMMON **FAULT:** SHE NOW AND THEN TOOK A DROP OF **GIN** OVERMUCH.

WHEN SHE WAS **FAST ASLEEP,** THE **MAD LADY** WOULD **TAKE** HER **KEYS** AND GO ROAMING ABOUT THE HOUSE, DOING **MISCHIEF.**

SHE *SET FIRE* TO THE *HANGINGS* OF THE *ROOM* NEXT TO HER *OWN*, AND *THEN* SHE MADE HER WAY TO THE *CHAMBER* THAT *HAD* BEEN THE *GOVERNESS'S*.

SHE WAS *LIKE* AS IF SHE *KNEW* SOMEHOW HOW MATTERS HAD *GONE ON*, AND HAD A *SPITE* AT HER;

BUT THERE WAS *NOBODY* SLEEPING IN IT, *FORTUNATELY*.

THE GOVERNESS HAD *RUN AWAY* TWO MONTHS *BEFORE*.

FOR ALL MR. ROCHESTER *SOUGHT* HER AS IF SHE HAD BEEN THE MOST *PRECIOUS* THING HE HAD IN THE *WORLD*, HE NEVER COULD HEAR A *WORD* OF HER; AND HE GREW *QUITE SAVAGE* IN HIS *DISAPPOINTMENT*:

HE NEVER *WAS* A *MILD* MAN, BUT HE GOT *DANGEROUS* AFTER HE *LOST* HER. HE WOULD BE ALONE, TOO.

HE SENT *MRS. FAIRFAX* THE HOUSEKEEPER AWAY TO HER FRIENDS; MISS *ADÈLE*, A WARD HE HAD, WAS PUT TO SCHOOL.

HE *BROKE OFF* ACQUAINTANCE WITH *ALL* THE *GENTRY*, AND *SHUT HIMSELF UP* LIKE A *HERMIT* AT THE HALL.

HE WOULD NOT *CROSS THE DOOR-STONES* OF THE *HOUSE*, EXCEPT AT *NIGHT*, WHEN HE WALKED LIKE A *GHOST* ABOUT THE GROUNDS AND IN THE ORCHARD AS IF HE HAD *LOST HIS SENSES*.

THEN MR. **ROCHESTER** WAS AT **HOME** WHEN THE **FIRE** BROKE OUT?

YES, *INDEED* WAS HE;

AND HE WENT UP TO THE *ATTICS* WHEN *ALL WAS BURNING* ABOVE AND *BELOW.*

HE GOT THE *SERVANTS* OUT OF THE BEDS AND HELPED THEM DOWN *HIMSELF.*

UH-
HUGG-
AHHCHH-
FAHG-
GRRR-
LLOCHLL-
BAHG!

AHHHH!

BERTHA!

FINALLY, HE WENT BACK TO GET HIS *MAD WIFE* OUT OF HER CELL. THEY *CALLED OUT* TO HIM THAT SHE WAS ON THE *ROOF.*

THE *NEXT* MINUTE SHE LAY *SMASHED* ON THE *PAVEMENT.*

DEAD?

AY, DEAD AS THE STONES ON WHICH HER *BRAINS* AND *BLOOD* WERE SCATTERED.

GOOD GOD!

YOU MAY WELL SAY SO, MA'AM: IT WAS *FRIGHTFUL!*

WERE **ANY OTHER** LIVES LOST?

NO – PERHAPS IT WOULD HAVE BEEN *BETTER* IF THERE *HAD.*

WHAT DO YOU *MEAN?*

POOR MR. EDWARD!

SOME SAY IT WAS A *JUST JUDGMENT* ON HIM FOR WANTING TO TAKE *ANOTHER WIFE* WHILE HE HAD ONE *LIVING;* BUT I *PITY* HIM, FOR MY PART.

YOU **SAID** HE WAS **ALIVE?**

YES: HE IS ALIVE; BUT *MANY* THINK HE HAD *BETTER* BE DEAD.

WHY? HOW? IS HE IN ENGLAND?

AY – AY – HE CAN'T *GET OUT OF* ENGLAND, I FANCY – – HE'S A *FIXTURE* NOW.

HE IS *STONE-BLIND,* IS MR. EDWARD.

I HAD DREADED WORSE. I DREADED HE WAS MAD.

IT WAS *ALL HIS OWN COURAGE,* AND A BODY MAY SAY, HIS *KINDNESS* IN A WAY, MA'AM. HE WOULDN'T LEAVE THE HOUSE TILL *EVERYONE* ELSE WAS OUT BEFORE HIM.

AS HE CAME DOWN THE GREAT STAIRCASE AT LAST, AFTER MRS. ROCHESTER HAD *FLUNG* HERSELF FROM THE *BATTLEMENTS,* THERE WAS A GREAT CRASH – ALL FELL.

RGHH!!

CRRAAASHH!!!

HE WAS *TAKEN OUT* FROM *UNDER* THE RUINS, ALIVE, BUT SADLY HURT.

ONE EYE WAS *KNOCKED OUT*, AND ONE HAND SO *CRUSHED* THAT MR. CARTER, THE SURGEON, HAD TO *AMPUTATE* IT DIRECTLY. THE *OTHER EYE* INFLAMED: HE LOST THE *SIGHT* OF THAT ALSO.

HE IS NOW *HELPLESS*, INDEED – *BLIND*, AND A *CRIPPLE*.

WHERE DOES HE LIVE *NOW?*

AT *FERNDEAN*, A MANOR HOUSE ON A *FARM* HE HAS, ABOUT THIRTY MILES OFF: QUITE A *DESOLATE* SPOT.

IF YOUR *POST-BOY* CAN *DRIVE ME THERE* BEFORE *DARK* THIS DAY, I'LL *PAY* BOTH *YOU* AND *HIM TWICE* THE HIRE YOU *USUALLY* DEMAND.

~ CHAPTER ~ ~ XXXVII~

MR. ROCHESTER OFTEN SPOKE OF FERNDEAN, AND SOMETIMES WENT THERE. HIS FATHER HAD PURCHASED THE ESTATE FOR THE SAKE OF THE GAME COVERS, BUT COULD FIND NO TENANT, IN CONSEQUENCE OF ITS INELIGIBLE AND INSALUBRIOUS SITE.

FERNDEAN THEN REMAINED UNINHABITED AND UNFURNISHED, WITH THE EXCEPTION OF SOME TWO OR THREE ROOMS FOR THE ACCOMMODATION OF THE SQUIRE WHEN HE WENT THERE IN THE SEASON TO SHOOT.

DUSK AS IT WAS, I RECOGNISED HIM.

I STAYED MY STEP, ALMOST MY BREATH, AND STOOD TO WATCH HIM - ALAS! TO HIM INVISIBLE. IT WAS A SUDDEN MEETING, AND ONE IN WHICH RAPTURE WAS KEPT WELL IN CHECK BY PAIN. I HAD NO DIFFICULTY IN RESTRAINING MY VOICE FROM EXCLAMATION, MY STEP FROM HASTY ADVANCE.

IN HIS COUNTENANCE, I SAW A CHANGE: THAT LOOKED DESPERATE AND BROODING - THAT REMINDED ME OF SOME WRONGED AND FETTERED WILD BEAST OR BIRD, DANGEROUS TO APPROACH IN HIS SULLEN WOE.

THE CAGED EAGLE, WHOSE GOLD-RINGED EYES CRUELTY HAS EXTINGUISHED, MIGHT LOOK AS LOOKED THAT SIGHTLESS SAMSON.

WILL YOU TAKE MY ARM, SIR? THERE IS A HEAVY SHOWER COMING ON. HAD YOU NOT BETTER GO IN?

LEAVE ME ALONE.

117

MR. ROCHESTER GROPED HIS WAY **BACK** TO THE **HOUSE** AND CLOSED THE **DOOR.** I NOW **DREW NEAR** AND **KNOCKED.**

MARY - HOW ARE YOU?

IS IT **REALLY** YOU, MISS, COME AT THIS **LATE HOUR** TO THIS **LONELY PLACE?**

RINGGGG!

WHEN YOU **GO IN,** TELL YOUR **MASTER** THAT A **PERSON** WISHES TO **SPEAK** TO HIM, BUT **DO NOT** GIVE MY **NAME.**

I **DON'T THINK** HE WILL **SEE** YOU. HE REFUSES **EVERYBODY.**

MOMENTS LATER...

YOU ARE TO **SEND IN** YOUR **NAME** AND YOUR **BUSINESS.**

IS **THAT** WHAT HE **RANG** FOR?

YES.

GIVE THE **TRAY** TO **ME;** I WILL **CARRY** IT IN.

Lie down!

YELP!

GIVE ME THE **WATER,** MARY.

118

QUITE RICH, SIR. I AM MY OWN MISTRESS.

AND YOU WILL STAY WITH ME?

CERTAINLY - UNLESS YOU OBJECT.

I WILL BE YOUR NEIGHBOUR, YOUR NURSE, YOUR HOUSEKEEPER, YOUR COMPANION - TO READ TO YOU, TO WALK WITH YOU, TO WAIT ON YOU, TO BE EYES AND HANDS TO YOU.

YOU SHALL NOT BE LEFT DESOLATE, SO LONG AS I LIVE.

YOU -- -- HAVE AN AFFECTIONATE HEART AND A GENEROUS SPIRIT, WHICH PROMPT YOU TO MAKE SACRIFICES FOR THOSE YOU PITY.

I SUPPOSE I SHOULD NOW ENTERTAIN NONE BUT FATHERLY FEELINGS FOR YOU:

DO YOU THINK SO? COME, TELL ME.

I WILL THINK WHAT YOU LIKE, SIR.

I AM CONTENT TO BE ONLY YOUR NURSE, IF YOU THINK IT BETTER.

BUT YOU CANNOT ALWAYS BE MY NURSE, *JANET: YOU ARE YOUNG - YOU MUST MARRY ONE DAY.

I DON'T CARE ABOUT BEING MARRIED.

YOU SHOULD CARE, JANET: IF I WERE WHAT I ONCE WAS, I WOULD TRY TO MAKE YOU CARE - BUT - A SIGHTLESS BLOCK!

HE RELAPSED AGAIN INTO GLOOM.

I RESUMED A LIVELIER VEIN OF CONVERSATION.

IT IS TIME SOMEONE UNDERTOOK TO REHUMANISE YOU, FOR I SEE YOU ARE BEING METAMORPHOSED INTO A LION.

YOUR HAIR REMINDS ME OF EAGLES' FEATHERS; WHETHER YOUR NAILS ARE GROWN LIKE BIRDS' CLAWS OR NOT, I HAVE NOT YET NOTICED.

ON THIS ARM, I HAVE NEITHER HAND NOR NAILS. IT IS A MERE STUMP - A GHASTLY SIGHT!

DON'T YOU THINK, JANE?

IT IS A PITY TO SEE IT; AND A PITY TO SEE YOUR EYES - AND THE SCAR OF FIRE ON YOUR FOREHEAD --

121

Mr. Rochester would sometimes call her Janet.

-- AND THE **WORST** OF IT IS, ONE IS IN **DANGER** OF **LOVING** YOU **TOO WELL** FOR ALL THIS, AND MAKING **TOO MUCH** OF YOU.

I **THOUGHT** YOU WOULD BE **REVOLTED**, JANE, WHEN YOU SAW MY **ARM**, AND MY **CICATRISED VISAGE**.

DID YOU? DON'T **TELL ME** SO - LEST I SHOULD **SAY** SOMETHING **DISPARAGING** ABOUT YOUR **JUDGMENT**.

NOW LET ME **LEAVE YOU** IN AN **INSTANT** TO MAKE A **BETTER FIRE**.

CAN YOU **TELL** WHEN THERE IS A **GOOD FIRE?**

YES; WITH THE **RIGHT EYE** I SEE A **GLOW** - A **RUDDY HAZE**.

AND YOU **SEE** THE **CANDLES?**

VERY **DIMLY** - EACH IS A **LUMINOUS CLOUD**.

CAN YOU SEE **ME?**

NO, MY **FAIRY**: BUT I AM **ONLY** TOO **THANKFUL** TO **HEAR** AND **FEEL YOU**.

WHEN DO YOU TAKE **SUPPER?**

I **NEVER** TAKE **SUPPER**.

BUT YOU **SHALL** HAVE SOME **TO-NIGHT**. I AM **HUNGRY**: SO ARE **YOU**, I **DARESAY**, ONLY YOU **FORGET**.

SUMMONING **MARY**, I SOON HAD THE **ROOM** IN MORE **CHEERFUL ORDER**: I **PREPARED** HIM, LIKEWISE, A **COMFORTABLE** REPAST. MY **SPIRITS** WERE **EXCITED**, AND WITH **PLEASURE** AND **EASE** I TALKED TO HIM DURING **SUPPER**, AND FOR A **LONG TIME** AFTER. WITH HIM I WAS AT **PERFECT EASE**, BECAUSE I **KNEW** I **SUITED** HIM; ALL I **SAID** OR **DID** SEEMED EITHER TO **CONSOLE** OR **REVIVE** HIM. IN HIS **PRESENCE** I **THOROUGHLY LIVED**; AND HE LIVED IN **MINE**.

IF A **MOMENT'S** SILENCE BROKE THE CONVERSATION, HE WOULD TURN **RESTLESS**, **TOUCH** ME, THEN SAY, "JANE".

YOU ARE **ALTOGETHER** A **HUMAN BEING**, JANE? YOU ARE **CERTAIN** OF THAT?

I **CONSCIENTIOUSLY** BELIEVE SO, MR. ROCHESTER.

HOW CAN IT **BE** THAT **JANE** IS WITH ME, AND SAYS SHE **LOVES** ME? WILL SHE NOT **DEPART** AS **SUDDENLY** AS SHE **CAME**?

TO-MORROW, I FEAR, I SHALL **FIND** HER NO **MORE**.

YOUR **EYEBROWS** ARE **SCORCHED**.

I WILL **APPLY** SOMETHING THAT WILL MAKE THEM **GROW** AS **BROAD** AND **BLACK** AS **EVER**.

WHERE IS THE **USE** OF DOING ME **GOOD** IN ANY WAY, BENEFICENT **SPIRIT**, WHEN, AT SOME **FATAL MOMENT**, YOU WILL AGAIN **DESERT** ME --

-- FOR **ME** REMAINING AFTERWARDS **UNDISCOVERABLE**?

HAVE YOU A **POCKET-COMB** ABOUT YOU, SIR, TO **COMB OUT** THIS **SHAGGY, BLACK MANE**?

I FIND YOU RATHER **ALARMING**, WHEN I **EXAMINE** YOU CLOSE AT **HAND**.

AM I **HIDEOUS**, JANE?

VERY, SIR; YOU ALWAYS **WERE**, YOU KNOW.

HUMPH! THE **WICKEDNESS** HAS NOT BEEN TAKEN OUT OF YOU, **WHEREVER** YOU HAVE SOJOURNED.

YET I HAVE **BEEN** WITH **GOOD PEOPLE** - **FAR** BETTER THAN **YOU**.

WHO THE **DEUCE** HAVE YOU **BEEN** WITH?

YOU SHALL **NOT** GET IT OUT OF ME **TO-NIGHT**, SIR; YOU MUST **WAIT** TILL **TO-MORROW**.

TO LEAVE MY TALE **HALF** TOLD **WILL**, YOU KNOW, BE A SORT OF **SECURITY** THAT I SHALL **APPEAR** AT YOUR **BREAKFAST-TABLE** TO **FINISH** IT.

YOU MOCKING CHANGELING - FAIRY-BORN AND HUMAN-BRED!

YOU MAKE ME FEEL AS I HAVE NOT FELT THESE TWELVE MONTHS.

NOW I'LL LEAVE YOU: I HAVE BEEN TRAVELLING THESE LAST THREE DAYS, AND I BELIEVE I AM TIRED.

JUST ONE WORD, JANE: WERE THERE ONLY LADIES IN THE HOUSE WHERE YOU HAVE BEEN?

HA-HA-HA!

A GOOD IDEA!

I SEE I HAVE THE MEANS OF FRETTING HIM OUT OF HIS MELANCHOLY FOR SOME TIME TO COME.

VERY EARLY THE NEXT MORNING, I HEARD HIM UP AND ASTIR, WANDERING FROM ONE ROOM TO ANOTHER.

GOOD MORNING, SIR.

IS MISS EYRE HERE?

WHICH ROOM DID YOU PUT HER INTO?

WAS IT DRY? IS SHE UP?

GO AND ASK HER IF SHE WANTS ANYTHING; AND WHEN SHE WILL COME DOWN.

IT IS A BRIGHT, SUNNY MORNING, SIR.

THE RAIN IS OVER AND GONE, AND THERE IS A TENDER SHINING AFTER IT; YOU SHALL HAVE A WALK SOON.

OH, YOU ARE INDEED THERE, MY SKYLARK!

I HEARD ONE OF YOUR KIND AN HOUR AGO, SINGING HIGH OVER THE WOOD: BUT ITS SONG HAD NO MUSIC FOR ME, ANY MORE THAN THE RISING SUN HAD RAYS.

ALL THE MELODY ON EARTH IS CONCENTRATED IN MY JANE'S TONGUE TO MY EAR - I AM GLAD IT IS NOT NATURALLY A SILENT ONE.

ALL THE SUNSHINE I CAN FEEL IS IN HER PRESENCE.

THE WATER STOOD IN MY EYES TO HEAR THIS AVOWAL OF HIS DEPENDENCE; JUST AS IF A ROYAL EAGLE, CHAINED TO A PERCH, MUST ENTREAT A SPARROW TO BECOME ITS PURVEYOR.

MOST OF THE MORNING WAS SPENT IN THE OPEN AIR.

CRUEL, CRUEL DESERTER!
OH JANE, WHAT DID I FEEL WHEN I DISCOVERED YOU HAD FLED FROM THORNFIELD, AND WHEN I COULD NOWHERE FIND YOU:
AND, AFTER EXAMINING YOUR APARTMENT, ASCERTAINED THAT YOU HAD TAKEN NO MONEY, NOR ANYTHING WHICH COULD SERVE AS AN EQUIVALENT!

WHAT COULD MY DARLING DO, I ASKED, LEFT DESTITUTE AND PENNILESS?

AND WHAT DID SHE DO? LET ME HEAR NOW.

THUS URGED, I BEGAN THE NARRATIVE OF MY EXPERIENCE FOR THE LAST YEAR. I SOFTENED CONSIDERABLY WHAT RELATED TO THE THREE DAYS OF WANDERING AND STARVATION; BECAUSE TO HAVE TOLD HIM ALL WOULD HAVE BEEN TO INFLICT UNNECESSARY PAIN.

I WOULD NEVER HAVE FORCED YOU TO BE MY MISTRESS.

I LOVE YOU FAR TOO WELL AND TOO TENDERLY TO BE YOUR TYRANT.

I WOULD HAVE GIVEN YOU HALF MY FORTUNE, WITHOUT DEMANDING SO MUCH AS A KISS IN RETURN, RATHER THAN HAVE YOU FLING YOURSELF FRIENDLESS ON THE WIDE WORLD.

YOU HAVE ENDURED, I AM CERTAIN, MORE THAN YOU HAVE CONFESSED TO ME.

WELL, WHATEVER MY SUFFERINGS HAD BEEN, THEY WERE VERY SHORT.

I THEN PROCEEDED TO TELL HIM HOW I HAD BEEN RECEIVED AT MOOR HOUSE; HOW I HAD OBTAINED THE OFFICE OF SCHOOL-MISTRESS, ETC.

OF COURSE, ST. JOHN RIVERS' NAME CAME IN FREQUENTLY IN THE PROGRESS OF MY TALE.

THIS ST. JOHN, THEN, IS YOUR COUSIN?

YES.

YOU HAVE SPOKEN OF HIM OFTEN: DO YOU LIKE HIM?

HE WAS A VERY GOOD MAN, SIR; I COULD NOT HELP LIKING HIM.

A GOOD MAN. DOES THAT MEAN A RESPECTABLE, WELL-CONDUCTED MAN OF FIFTY? OR WHAT DOES IT MEAN?

ST. JOHN WAS ONLY TWENTY-NINE, SIR.

JEUNE ENCORE. IS HE OF LOW STATURE, PHLEGMATIC, AND PLAIN?

IS HIS BRAIN SOFT? HE MEANS WELL: BUT YOU SHRUG YOUR SHOULDERS TO HEAR HIM TALK?

ST. JOHN MADE YOU SCHOOL-MISTRESS OF MORTON **BEFORE** HE KNEW YOU WERE HIS **COUSIN**?

YES.

YOU WOULD **OFTEN** SEE HIM AT **YOUR COTTAGE** NEAR THE **SCHOOL**?

NOW AND THEN. HE **STUDIED** A GOOD DEAL.

DID HE TEACH **YOU** ANYTHING?

A LITTLE **HINDOSTANEE**.

OF WHAT **USE** COULD HINDOSTANEE BE TO **YOU**?

HE **INTENDED** ME TO **GO WITH HIM** TO INDIA.

AH! **HERE** I REACH THE **ROOT** OF THE MATTER. HE **WANTED** YOU TO **MARRY HIM**?

HE **ASKED** ME TO MARRY HIM.

THAT IS A **FICTION** - AN IMPUDENT INVENTION TO VEX ME.

I BEG YOUR **PARDON**, IT IS THE **LITERAL TRUTH**:

HE **ASKED** ME **MORE** THAN **ONCE**, AND WAS AS **STIFF** ABOUT **URGING** HIS **POINT** AS **EVER YOU** COULD BE.

MISS EYRE, I **REPEAT** IT, YOU **CAN LEAVE ME**. **WHY** DO YOU REMAIN PERTINACIOUSLY **PERCHED** ON MY **KNEE**, WHEN I HAVE **GIVEN** YOU **NOTICE** TO **QUIT**?

BECAUSE I AM **COMFORTABLE** THERE.

NO, JANE, YOU ARE **NOT** COMFORTABLE THERE, BECAUSE YOUR **HEART** IS **NOT** WITH **ME**:

IT IS WITH THIS **COUSIN** - THIS **ST. JOHN**.

OH, TILL THIS **MOMENT**, I **THOUGHT** MY LITTLE **JANE** WAS **ALL MINE**!

SHAKE ME **OFF**, THEN, SIR, FOR I'LL **NOT** LEAVE YOU OF MY **OWN ACCORD**.

HE IS **NOT** MY **HUSBAND**, NOR **EVER** WILL BE.

HE **DOES NOT LOVE ME**: I DO NOT LOVE HIM.

HE **LOVES** - AS HE **CAN** LOVE, AND **THAT** IS **NOT** AS **YOU** LOVE - A **BEAUTIFUL YOUNG LADY** CALLED **ROSAMOND**.

HE WANTED TO MARRY ME **ONLY** BECAUSE HE THOUGHT I SHOULD MAKE A SUITABLE **MISSIONARY'S WIFE**, WHICH **SHE** WOULD **NOT** HAVE DONE.

HITHERTO, I HAVE **HATED** TO BE **HELPED** - TO BE **LED**. BUT IT IS **PLEASANT** TO FEEL MY **HAND** CIRCLED BY JANE'S LITTLE **FINGERS**.

JANE **SUITS** ME: DO **I** SUIT **HER**?

TO THE **FINEST FIBRE** OF MY **NATURE**, SIR.

THE CASE BEING **SO**, WE HAVE **NOTHING** IN THE **WORLD** TO **WAIT** FOR: WE MUST BE **MARRIED INSTANTLY**.

JANE! YOU **THINK** ME, I **DARESAY**, AN **IRRELIGIOUS DOG**: BUT MY **HEART** SWELLS WITH **GRATITUDE** TO THE **BENEFICENT GOD** OF THIS **EARTH** JUST NOW.

OF **LATE** - ONLY OF LATE - I **BEGAN** TO SEE THE **HAND** OF GOD IN MY **DOOM**. I BEGAN TO EXPERIENCE **REMORSE**, **REPENTANCE**; I BEGAN **SOMETIMES** TO **PRAY**.

LAST **MONDAY** NIGHT, A **SINGULAR MOOD** CAME OVER ME: ONE IN WHICH **GRIEF** REPLACED **FRENZY**. I HAD **LONG** HAD THE **IMPRESSION** THAT SINCE I COULD **NOWHERE FIND** YOU, YOU **MUST** BE **DEAD**.

LATE THAT **NIGHT**, I **SUPPLICATED** GOD, THAT, IF IT SEEMED **GOOD** TO HIM, I MIGHT **SOON** BE **TAKEN** FROM THIS **LIFE**; AND ADMITTED TO **THAT WORLD** TO **COME**, WHERE THERE WAS **STILL HOPE** OF **REJOINING JANE**.

I **LONGED** FOR THEE, **JANET!** BOTH WITH **SOUL** AND **FLESH!**

THE **ALPHA** AND **OMEGA** OF MY **HEART'S** WISHES BROKE **INVOLUNTARILY** FROM MY **LIPS** IN THE **WORDS...**

JANE! JANE! JANE!

DID YOU **SPEAK** THESE **WORDS** ALOUD?

I **DID**, JANE. IF ANY **LISTENER** HAD **HEARD** ME, HE WOULD HAVE THOUGHT ME **MAD**, I **PRONOUNCED** THEM WITH SUCH **FRANTIC ENERGY**.

AND IT WAS **LAST MONDAY** NIGHT, SOMEWHERE NEAR **MIDNIGHT**?

YES; BUT THE **TIME** IS OF **NO CONSEQUENCE**: WHAT **FOLLOWED** IS THE **STRANGE POINT**.

129

YOU WILL **THINK** ME **SUPERSTITIOUS**. A **VOICE** - I CANNOT **TELL** WHENCE THE VOICE **CAME**, BUT I **KNOW** WHOSE **VOICE** IT WAS - REPLIED...

I AM COMING: WAIT FOR ME...

WHERE ARE YOU?

AND A **MOMENT AFTER**, WENT **WHISPERING** ON THE **WIND** THE WORDS...

COOLER AND **FRESHER** AT THE **MOMENT** THE GALE SEEMED TO **VISIT** MY **BROW**: I COULD HAVE **DEEMED** THAT IN SOME **WILD, LONE SCENE**, I AND JANE WERE **MEETING**.

IN **SPIRIT**, I BELIEVE WE **MUST** HAVE MET. **YOU** NO DOUBT WERE; AT THAT **HOUR**, IN **UNCONSCIOUS SLEEP**, JANE:

PERHAPS YOUR **SOUL WANDERED** FROM ITS **CELL TO COMFORT** MINE; FOR THOSE WERE **YOUR** ACCENTS, AS **CERTAIN** AS I **LIVE**, THEY WERE **YOURS!**

IT WAS ON **MONDAY NIGHT** - NEAR **MIDNIGHT** - THAT I **TOO** HAD RECEIVED THE **MYSTERIOUS SUMMONS**: THOSE WERE THE **VERY WORDS** BY WHICH I **REPLIED** TO IT.

I MADE **NO DISCLOSURE** IN **RETURN**: MY **TALE** WOULD MAKE A **PROFOUND IMPRESSION** ON THE **MIND** OF MY **HEARER**: AND **THAT** MIND, YET FROM ITS **SUFFERINGS** TOO PRONE TO **GLOOM**, NEEDED **NOT** THE **DEEPER SHADE** OF THE **SUPERNATURAL**.

YOU **CANNOT** NOW **WONDER** THAT WHEN YOU **ROSE** UPON ME SO **UNEXPECTEDLY** LAST NIGHT, I HAD DIFFICULTY IN **BELIEVING** YOU ANY **OTHER** THAN A **MERE VOICE** AND **VISION**,

SOMETHING THAT WOULD **MELT** TO **SILENCE** AND **ANNIHILATION**, AS THE **MIDNIGHT WHISPER** AND **MOUNTAIN ECHO** HAD MELTED **BEFORE**.

NOW, I THANK **GOD**! I **KNOW** IT TO BE **OTHERWISE**. YES, I THANK **GOD**!

I THANK MY **MAKER**, THAT, IN THE **MIDST** OF **JUDGMENT**, HE HAS **REMEMBERED MERCY**.

I HUMBLY **ENTREAT** MY **REDEEMER** TO GIVE ME **STRENGTH** TO LEAD HENCEFORTH A **PURER** LIFE THAN I HAVE DONE **HITHERTO**!

THEN HE STRETCHED HIS **HAND OUT** TO BE **LED**.

I **TOOK** THAT **DEAR HAND, HELD** IT A MOMENT TO MY **LIPS**, THEN LET IT PASS ROUND MY **SHOULDER**: BEING SO MUCH **LOWER** OF **STATURE** THAN HE, I SERVED BOTH FOR HIS **PROP** AND **GUIDE**. WE ENTERED THE **WOOD**, AND WENDED **HOMEWARD**.

~ CHAPTER ~ ~ XXXVIII ~ CONCLUSION

I **MARRIED HIM**. A **QUIET** WEDDING, WE HAD: HE AND I, THE **PARSON** AND **CLERK**, WERE **ALONE PRESENT**. I WROTE TO **MOOR HOUSE** AND TO **CAMBRIDGE** IMMEDIATELY, TO SAY WHAT I HAD **DONE**: FULLY EXPLAINING ALSO **WHY** I HAD THUS ACTED.

DIANA AND MARY APPROVED THE STEP **UNRESERVEDLY**.

DIANA SAYS THAT SHE WILL **JUST** GIVE ME **TIME** TO GET OVER THE **HONEYMOON**, AND THEN SHE WILL **COME** AND **SEE** ME!

SHE HAD **BETTER NOT WAIT** TILL **THEN**, JANE. IF SHE **DOES**, SHE WILL BE **TOO LATE**, FOR OUR **HONEYMOON** WILL **SHINE** OUR **LIFE LONG**:

ITS **BEAMS** WILL ONLY **FADE** OVER **YOUR GRAVE** OR MINE.

HOW **ST. JOHN** RECEIVED THE NEWS, I **DON'T** KNOW:

HE NEVER ANSWERED THE **LETTER** IN WHICH I **COMMUNICATED** IT.

YET SIX MONTHS **AFTER** HE **WROTE** TO ME, **WITHOUT**, HOWEVER, MENTIONING MR. **ROCHESTER'S NAME** OR **ALLUDING** TO MY **MARRIAGE**. HIS **LETTER** WAS THEN **CALM**, AND, THOUGH VERY **SERIOUS**, KIND.

HE HAS MAINTAINED A **REGULAR**, THOUGH NOT **FREQUENT**, CORRESPONDENCE EVER **SINCE**.

I HAVE **NOW** BEEN MARRIED **TEN YEARS.** I **KNOW** WHAT IT IS TO LIVE ENTIRELY **FOR** AND **WITH** WHAT I **LOVE BEST ON EARTH.** I **HOLD** MYSELF **SUPREMELY BLEST -** **BLEST BEYOND** WHAT **LANGUAGE** CAN **EXPRESS;** BECAUSE I AM MY HUSBAND'S LIFE AS **FULLY** AS HE IS **MINE.**

MR. **ROCHESTER** CONTINUED **BLIND** THE **FIRST** TWO YEARS OF OUR UNION. ONE **MORNING...**

JANE, HAVE YOU A **GLITTERING ORNAMENT** ROUND YOUR NECK? AND HAVE YOU A **PALE BLUE DRESS** ON?

YES!

FOR **SOME TIME,** I HAVE **FANCIED** THAT THE **OBSCURITY** CLOUDING **ONE EYE** WAS BECOMING **LESS DENSE;** NOW I AM **SURE** OF IT.

HE AND I WENT UP TO **LONDON.** HE HAD THE **ADVICE** OF AN **EMINENT OCULIST;** AND HE **EVENTUALLY RECOVERED** THE **SIGHT** OF THAT **ONE EYE.**

HE HAS **MY EYES** AS THEY **ONCE** WERE.

YES - SO **LARGE, BLACK** AND **BRILLIANT.**

I **THANK GOD,** WHO HAS **AGAIN** TEMPERED **JUDGMENT** WITH **MERCY.**

DIANA AND **MARY** RIVERS ARE BOTH **MARRIED:** ALTERNATELY, ONCE EVERY **YEAR,** THEY COME TO SEE **US,** AND **WE** GO TO SEE THEM. DIANA'S HUSBAND IS A **CAPTAIN** IN THE **NAVY;** MARY'S IS A **CLERGYMAN.**

ST. JOHN RIVERS WENT TO **INDIA.** HE ENTERED ON THE **PATH** HE **MARKED** FOR HIMSELF. HE IS **UNMARRIED:** HE **NEVER WILL** MARRY NOW. HIS GLORIOUS **SUN** HASTENS TO ITS **SETTING.** I KNOW THA A **STRANGER'S** HAND WILL WRITE TO ME NEXT, TO SAY THAT THE **GOOD** AND **FAITHFUL** SERVANT HAS BEEN CALLED AT **LENGTH** INTO THE **JOY** OF HIS **LORD.**

AND WHY **WEEP** FOR THIS? NO **FEAR** OF **DEATH** WILL DARKEN ST. JOHN'S LAST HOUR

HIS **MIND** WILL BE **UNCLOUDED,** HIS **HEART** WILL BE **UNDAUNTED,** HIS **HOPE** WILL BE **SURE,** AND HIS **FAITH STEADFAST.**

132

Jane Eyre

The End

Charlotte Brontë

(1816 –1855)

"Literature cannot be the business of a woman's life..."

Poet Laureate Robert Southeys' letter to Charlotte Brontë in 1837

George Richmond, chalk, 1850 National Portrait Gallery, London

Charlotte Brontë was born on April 21, 1816, at 74 Market Street in the village of Thornton near Bradford, Yorkshire, in the north of England. She was one of six children born to Maria Branwell and Patrick Brontë: Maria (1814), Elizabeth (1815), Charlotte (1816), Patrick Branwell (who was known as Branwell, 1817), Emily (1818) and Anne (1820).

Her father, Patrick, was an Irish Anglican clergyman and writer, born in County Down, Ireland, in 1777. His surname was originally Brunty, but he decided to change his name, probably to give the impression of a more well-to-do background, giving the world the now familiar "Brontë." Charlotte's mother, Maria, was born in 1785, to a prosperous merchant family in Cornwall. Patrick and Maria met in Hartshead, Yorkshire, while she was helping her aunt with the domestic side of running a school.

In April 1820, when Charlotte was four years old, the family moved a short distance from Thornton to Haworth, where Patrick had been appointed perpetual curate of the church. Maria's sister, Elizabeth joined them a year later to help look after the children and to care for her sister, who was suffering from the final stages of cancer. She died in September 1821 – Charlotte was still only five years old.

The Parsonage at Haworth was a literary household. From early childhood, the Brontë children had written about the lives, wars and sufferings of people who lived in their own imaginary kingdoms. The story goes that Branwell had been given a set of toy soldiers in June 1826, and from these the children developed imaginary worlds of their own. Charlotte and Branwell wrote stories about their country — **"Angria"** — and Emily and Anne wrote articles and poems about theirs — **"Gondal"**. These sagas, plays, poems and stories were written down in handmade "little books" – books that they made from paper sheets stitched together. In a letter to author and biographer Elizabeth Gaskell, Patrick Brontë wrote:

> **"When mere children, as soon as they could read and write, Charlotte and her brother and sisters used to invent and act little plays of their own."**

In July 1824 Maria (ten) and Elizabeth (nine) were sent to the Clergy Daughter's School at Cowan Bridge, near Kirkby Lonsdale in Lancashire (about 45 miles away from their home). Charlotte (eight) and Emily (six) joined them there in August. Life at boarding school must have been grim. Maria became ill and was sent home in February 1825; she died at Haworth in May. Elizabeth fell ill that same month and, like her sister, was sent home; she died just a few months later. Both sisters died of tuberculosis (also known as "consumption") and as a result of their deaths, Emily and Charlotte were withdrawn from the school. These events obviously had a great impact on Charlotte, who drew on the experience for *Jane Eyre* when she described Lowood School and the death of Helen Burns.

In fact much of the novel mirrors Charlotte's own life. Charlotte, like Jane, spent many years as a governess for a number of families - a career which she viewed with some distaste (a view which appears in Chapter 30 of this book, at the bottom of page 95). Having no personal fortune and few respectable ways of earning a living, this was the only socially acceptable option for many genteel young ladies. Emily and Anne also became governesses, although Emily's career as a teacher was short-lived; it is reported that she told her pupils at Miss Patchett's School in Halifax that she much preferred the school dog to any of them!

In 1842, Charlotte and Emily traveled to Brussels to study at the Pensionnat Heger — a boarding school run by Constantin Heger and his wife. Their Aunt Elizabeth Branwell paid for this trip, with the plan that they would set up their own school at the Parsonage when they returned. However, the girls were forced to return to England later that year when their Aunt Elizabeth died — just as in this book when Jane Eyre returns to Gateshead Hall when her Aunt Reed is on her death-bed.

Charlotte traveled alone to Brussels in January 1843 to take up a teaching post at Pensionnat Heger. This second stay was not a happy one: she was lonely without her sister, homesick, and had become deeply attached to Constantin Heger. She returned to Haworth a year later in January 1844. Her time at Pensionnat Heger became the inspiration for parts of two other books: *The Professor* and *Villette;* and her attraction to the married Constantin would seem to reflect Jane Eyre's love for Mr. Rochester.

Of the three sisters, Anne was the most successful teacher; but by 1845 the entire family, including Branwell, were all back at The Parsonage. Branwell returned home somewhat in disgrace for "proceedings bad beyond expression" — most likely a love affair with his employer's wife.

After Charlotte's return home, the sisters finally started on their project to start a school of their own. This turned out to be a total failure — they didn't manage to attract a single student! However that was probably to the world's advantage. Over the years, the sisters had continued their writing, and in 1846 — having abandoned the idea of starting a school - they decided to publish a selection of their poems. The title was simply *Poems* and it was published under different author names: Currer (Charlotte), Ellis (Emily) and Acton (Anne) Bell. One thousand copies of the book were printed, at a cost of around $100, which they funded themselves. The book received some favorable reviews, but sold only two copies in the first year.

Charlotte gave an explanation for these pseudonyms:

> "Averse to personal publicity, we veiled our own names under those of Currer, Ellis and Acton Bell; the ambiguous choice being dictated by a sort of conscientious scruple at assuming Christian names positively masculine, while we did not like to declare ourselves women, because – without at that time suspecting that our mode of writing and thinking was not what is called 'feminine' – we had a vague impression that authoresses are liable to be looked on with prejudice; we had noticed how critics sometimes use for their chastisement the weapon of personality, and for their reward, a flattery, which is not true praise."

In the same year that *Poems* was published, Charlotte also completed her first novel, *The Professor*. It was rejected by a number of publishers, but despite that, Charlotte remained undeterred. The following year saw the publication of Charlotte's *Jane Eyre*, Emily's *Wuthering Heights*, and Anne's *Agnes Grey*; all published under their assumed "Bell" names.

The sisters hid behind their assumed names until 1848, when Anne's second novel, *The Tenant of Wildfell Hall* was published; and the sisters were forced to reveal their true identities.

These first successes for the sisters were overshadowed by sadness. Their brother, Branwell, had been subjecting himself to alcohol and opium abuse for many years; and he died in 1848 – officially from tuberculosis, but thought to be brought on by his drug and drink habits. He was just thirty-one years old.

At the same time, Anne and Emily both became ill with tuberculosis. Emily died in December 1848, aged thirty.

Charlotte took Anne (who was now her only sibling) to the coastal town of Scarborough in May 1849, hoping that the sea air would help to cure her. Unfortunately, Anne died just four days after their arrival, aged only twenty-nine. She was buried in Scarborough so that their father didn't have to suffer the pain of yet another family funeral.

Shortly afterwards, Charlotte wrote:

"A year ago – had a prophet warned me how I should stand in June 1849 – how stripped and bereaved....I should have thought – this can never be endured..."

Charlotte turned to her writing for comfort in these bleak times; and her next novel, *Shirley* was published in October 1849. She was now quite famous and attracted a great deal of attention. For instance, during one of her many visits to London she not only met her literary idol, W.M. Thackeray, but she also had her portrait painted by popular High Society artist George Richmond (reproduced at the top of page 134).

Her next novel, *Villette* published in 1853, was to be her last.

During this time, Charlotte had also attracted the personal attention of her father's curate, the Reverend Arthur Bell Nicholls. Charlotte initially rejected Reverend Nicholls' proposal for marriage,

probably due to her father thinking that he was not worthy of his now-famous daughter. Eventually, however, he softened, and Charlotte married Reverend Nicholls in Haworth Church on June 29, 1854, and they spent their honeymoon in Ireland. Once again, this is mirrored in *Jane Eyre*, where Jane attracts the interest of a religious man, and also where Mr. Rochester suggests sending her away to Ireland. More interestingly, however, these actual events took place after *Jane Eyre* was written!

Charlotte became pregnant; and at the same time, her health began to decline. Elizabeth Gaskell, Charlotte's earliest biographer, writes that she was attacked by

"sensations of perpetual nausea and ever-recurring faintness."

Charlotte and her unborn child died on March 31, 1855, three weeks before her thirty-ninth birthday. Her death certificate gives the cause of death as phthisis (tuberculosis).

Her husband, Reverend Nicholls, looked after Charlotte's father, Patrick, for six years until his death in June 1861 at the age of eighty-four.

Other than Patrick, none of the Brontës of Haworth enjoyed a long life, and none of them had any children to carry on the literary name.

"Gentle, soft dream, nestling in my arms now, you will fly, too, as your sisters have all fled before you:"

(from Jane Eyre, written while her younger sisters were alive).

The Brontë Family Tree

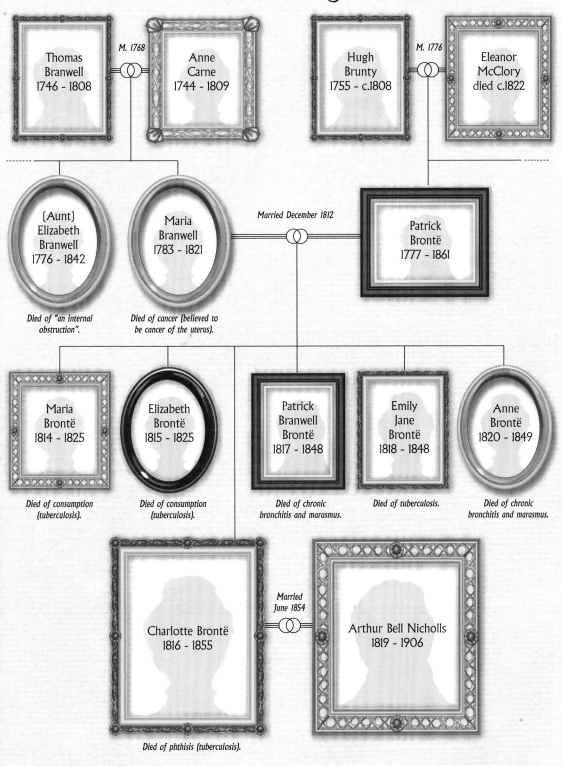

Thomas Branwell 1746 - 1808

M. 1768

Anne Carne 1744 - 1809

Hugh Brunty 1755 - c.1808

M. 1776

Eleanor McClory died c.1822

(Aunt) Elizabeth Branwell 1776 - 1842

Died of "an internal obstruction".

Maria Branwell 1783 - 1821

Died of cancer (believed to be cancer of the uterus).

Married December 1812

Patrick Brontë 1777 - 1861

Maria Brontë 1814 - 1825

Died of consumption (tuberculosis).

Elizabeth Brontë 1815 - 1825

Died of consumption (tuberculosis).

Patrick Branwell Brontë 1817 - 1848

Died of chronic bronchitis and marasmus.

Emily Jane Brontë 1818 - 1848

Died of tuberculosis.

Anne Brontë 1820 - 1849

Died of chronic bronchitis and marasmus.

Charlotte Brontë 1816 - 1855

Died of phthisis (tuberculosis).

Married June 1854

Arthur Bell Nicholls 1819 - 1906

Key:
Parent of ————
Married ══◯◯══

Due to the lack of official records of births, deaths and marriages within this period, the above information is derived from extensive research and is as accurate as possible from the limited sources available.

137

A Chronology

1816   **April 21:** Charlotte is born at Thornton, Yorkshire, England, the third daughter of Patrick Brontë and Maria Branwell Brontë.

1817   **June 26:** Patrick Branwell Brontë is born.

1818   **July 30:** Emily Jane Brontë is born.

1820   **January 17:** Anne Brontë is born.

       February: Patrick Senior is appointed curate at Haworth.

       April: the Brontë family moves to Haworth.

1821   **September:** Maria Brontë dies of cancer. Her sister, Elizabeth Branwell, moves in with the family.

1824   **July:** Elizabeth and Maria are sent to the Clergy Daughters' School at Cowan Bridge, Lancashire.

       August: Charlotte and Emily are also sent to the Clergy Daughters' School (the school became a model for Lowood School in Jane Eyre).

1825   Elizabeth and Maria both return home from school in ill health. Maria dies in May, Elizabeth dies in June (both from tuberculosis, or "consumption"). Charlotte and Emily are removed from the school and sent home.

1826-1831   To entertain themselves, the children fill the pages of miniature homemade books with stories about imaginary kingdoms, inspired by some toy soldiers given to Branwell as a gift.

1831   **January:** Charlotte attends Miss Wooler's school at Roe Head, Mirfield. Here she meets lifelong friends Mary Taylor and Ellen Nussey.

1832   **June:** Charlotte leaves Roe Head to return home and teach her sisters.

1835   **July:** Charlotte returns to Roe Head as a teacher, taking Emily with her as a free pupil.

       October: Emily returns home, and Anne takes her place.

1838   **December:** Charlotte resigns her position and returns to Haworth.

1839   **March:** Charlotte rejects a marriage proposal from Reverend Henry Nussey, Ellen's brother.

       May to July: Charlotte works as a governess in Lothersdale.

       July: Charlotte rejects another marriage proposal, this time from Mr. Pryce — an Irish curate.

1841   Charlotte works as a governess at Rawdon from March to December.

1842   **February:** Charlotte and Emily go to Brussels to study languages at the Pensionnat Heger.

       October: Their Aunt Elizabeth dies.

       November: Charlotte and Emily return to Haworth.

1843   **January:** Charlotte returns to Brussels alone, but is lonely and becomes depressed. She forms an attachment to Constantin Heger, the head of the school, whose intellect appeals to her. Madame Heger's jealousy necessitates her departure.

1844   With all of the siblings now back at Haworth, the family try to start a school at the Haworth parsonage, but it is not a success.

1845   The Reverend Arthur Bell Nicholls becomes curate at Haworth.

1846   **April:** Charlotte, Emily, and Anne publish at their own expense a joint volume of *Poems* by Currer, Ellis, and Acton Bell. Only two copies are sold. Charlotte's novel *The Professor* is rejected by publishers.

       August: Charlotte begins *Jane Eyre* while caring for her father who was recovering from an eye operation.

1847   **October:** *Jane Eyre* is published, and is an immediate success. It starts off life as *Jane Eyre: An Autobiography Edited by Currer Bell* as if Jane Eyre was a real person and Charlotte Brontë, working under her assumed name of Currer Bell was merely the editor.

1848   **September:** Charlotte starts *Shirley*; Branwell dies of tuberculosis.

       December: Emily dies of tuberculosis. Anne also becomes ill.

1849   **May:** Charlotte tries to nurse Anne back to health and takes her to Scarborough. She dies four days after they arrive there.

       October: *Shirley – A Tale by Currer Bell* is published.

1849-1851   Charlotte travels frequently. She is invited to London as the guest of her publisher, where she meets Thackeray.

       She also visits the Lake District, Scotland, and Manchester, where she meets with Elizabeth Gaskell, her future biographer.

1851   **April:** She rejects a marriage proposal from James Taylor, a member of her publishing house.

1853   **January:** *Villette*, a novel set in Brussels is published, still by Currer Bell.

1854   **June:** Charlotte marries her fourth suitor, Arthur Bell Nichols, her father's curate. She begins but does not finish a novel, *Emma*.

1855   **March:** Charlotte dies during her pregnancy and is buried at The Parsonage at Haworth.

1857   **March:** Elizabeth Gaskell's *The Life of Charlotte Brontë* is published.

       June: Her previously rejected novel *The Professor* is published posthumously.

A Letter from Charlotte

This is a letter written by Charlotte Brontë on September 24, 1847 to her publisher, Messrs. Smith, Elder and Co., thanking them for their punctuation of her manuscript for *Jane Eyre*. Interestingly, she signs it as C. Bell, which was the name under which she wrote *Jane Eyre* (see page 135). Seeing the finished book today, it is hard to imagine a time when the classic tale didn't exist; but like any other work, it had to be conceived and written. This letter, then, is like a time capsule - linking us back to when the book was still a work-in-progress:

"Gentlemen,

I have to thank you for punctuating the sheets before sending them to me as I found the task very puzzling - and besides I consider your mode of punctuation a great deal mo[re] correct and rational than my own.

I am glad you think pretty well of the first part of "*Jane Eyre*" and I trust, for both your sakes and my own the public may think pretty well of it too.

Henceforth I hope that I shall be able to return the sheets promptly and regularly.

I am Gentlemen
Yours respectfully
C Bell"

To Messrs. Smith, Elder and Co.,
September 24th (1847)

Page Creation

In order to create two versions of the same book, the story is first adapted into two scripts: Original Text and Quick Text. While the degree of complexity changes for each script, the artwork remains the same for both books.

A page from the script of *Jane Eyre* showing the two versions of text.

The pencil drawing of page 91.

Jane Eyre artist John M. Burns guides us through the creation process:

"First off, I make A5-ish thumbnails of the page layout. These are transferred to the art board which is then masked with tape while at the same time making any alterations to the page layout.

I then start the finished pencil drawings.

The rough sketch created from the above script.

The next process is to ink these drawings. For Jane Eyre I mixed the ink I used (black, yellow ochre, and burnt umber). This gives the drawings a slight period look and is not such a contrast as black.

The ink drawing in this case is more a guide for the color. However I will work up an inked drawing if I feel a flat color will work.

After the ink stage the fun begins (the painting)."

The inked image, ready for coloring.

Adding color brings the page and its characters to life.

Each character has a detailed Character Study drawn. This is useful for the artist to refer to and ensures continuity throughout the book.

Jane Eyre character study

The final stage is to add the captions, sound effects, and dialogue speech bubbles from the script. These are laid on top of the colored pages. Two versions of each page are lettered, one for each of the two versions of the book (Original Text and Quick Text).

These are then saved as final artwork pages and compiled into the finished book.

Original Text

ISBN:
978-1-906332-47-1

THE CLASSIC NOVEL
BROUGHT TO LIFE IN FULL COLOR!

Quick Text

ISBN:
978-1-906332-48-8

THE FULL STORY IN QUICK MODERN
ENGLISH FOR A FAST-PACED READ!